GODS AND MONSTERS

CARNIVAL OF MYSTERIES

RACHEL LANGELLA

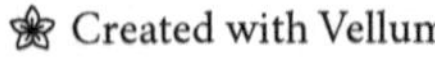 Created with Vellum

For Kevin L. Craig
Thanks for all the love and support

and

For Kendra Patterson
Thanks for helping us keep the faith!

CONTENTS

FOREWORD

A few years ago, Rachel Langella and I had an idea. It was, as book ideas go, one that we thought was really good. What if we had this carnival that went from place to place, and at each stop we had a new romance? We could have all these background characters, and the Carnival itself would be very mysterious and magical. We pictured it being a multi-book series that would probably take us years to write, but maybe we could do one or two books a year to keep it going.

Then the great global pandemic happened, and our writing mojo sort of tanked. We found it almost impossible to put out a single book per year, much less the six or more we'd been doing previously.

But that didn't mean our idea wasn't still really cool, so, we thought, why not open it up to a bunch of other authors, the way Meghan Maslow had opened up the Magical Emporium to us? That way it wouldn't be wasted, and we'd get the fun of reading some of our favorite author's takes on our idea. We weren't sure at first that anyone would be interested, but... wow. The interest was HUGE, so big that we had to turn away several authors because it was becoming more than I felt capable of managing. I CAN herd cats -- er, authors -- but it has to be below a certain number just for my own sanity. And it worked!

It's been a heck of a ride, really, but I've loved the result. There's something at the Carnival for every taste, or at least we hope so!

Of course a series like this doesn't happen without a lot of help. First, the authors, who worked their butts off to give us such great stories. Then there is the amazing Dianne Theis, who did all the covers. They are, in my humble opinion, some of the most beautiful and unique covers I've ever seen, and myself and the rest of the authors love them. Then we have all the editors, ARC readers, reviewers (thank you, Paranormal Romance Guild!) and fans who have supported us and made this possible. Thank you to everyone, this has been the realization of a dream, to see our idea brought to life!

And I would be remiss if I didn't acknowledge our influences in bringing this to life. First and foremost is the series Carnivale, which Rachel and I watched years ago and absolutely adored -- and for more reasons than just our shared love of Clancy Brown. While our acts are different, of course, it was the feel, the magic both good and ill in that carnival that helped to shape ours.

Then there are all the multiverse stories from the authors that Rachel and I grew up reading, probably starting with H.G. Wells, then Andre Norton, Madeleine L'Engle, C.S. Lewis, and of course Heinlein's Number of the Beast/Pursuit of the Pankera, one of the ultimate multiverse traveling books. All of these had some part to play, and there are more than a few tributes to famous books and movies in Gods and Monsters. I hope you have a good time trying to find them all!

Thanks for reading the series, and our own humble contribution.

Love, Ari

PROLOGUE

Errante walked along the edge of the Carnival, footsteps silent on the night-damp grass. Above him, the stars shone in a field of black, their true colors muted. The night wind was soft on his face, and he closed his eyes, breathing deeply of the lingering scents of the day, overlaid with the evergreen tang of the nearby forest. His task on this world was done, another Traveler delivered to the place they needed to be along their Path. Around him the world slept, then paused. Overhead, a bright moon shone, its power flowing into him until he glowed. It was time.

Slowly, he let his awareness expand.

He could feel each soul of the Carnival, human, inhuman, animal, mortal and immortal, living and not. These were his friends, who had become his family as well. In this moment and place, he was alone, yet not, for even now they were with him, cocooned in his magic, safe within its protection. The sleepers dreamed their dreams, every breath and slumberous thought forging in their Paths. He could sense those trails, spreading out like a spiderweb into the ether, and he chose the brightest one, the one that shone like the beam of a lighthouse reaching toward a tempest-tossed ship at sea. Yes, that one, there! It beckoned like a siren, showing him where they needed to go. He'd rarely seen one so focused and certain. What he would find there, he knew not, but he sensed its rightness with the certainty of all that he was.

Throwing back his arms, he called the Path. The power within him woke to his command, and he opened his eyes, watching as the Carnival shifted and became a swirl of light engulfing him, one that he wore like a cloak over a body no longer corporeal. The world where they had been dropped away, and now the stars blazed around him in colors no human had ever seen, bright and unimpeded by atmosphere. The cosmos was all around him, the towering, cloudy nebulas birthing new stars as he watched. Black holes devoured entire solar systems, and quasars sped away along their courses in streaks of red-shifted light, heading toward some unknown fate at the edge of the all existence. He and the Carnival were now separate from time and space. Had he wished, he could have traveled back to the dawn of the universe, or forward to its inevitable death and rebirth.

This was part of his unique magic. He was the Traveler, the Wanderer, able to be everywhere and yet nowhere, always and never, anyplace that souls existed or would exist. But now was not the time for his own explorations, not when there was another who needed his help to Travel their own Path. Focusing on his goal, he took a single step. The cosmos shifted as he crossed whole galaxies, light blurring into streaks at the speed of his passage. Then the next step found him on solid ground once more.

The swirl of light he wore expanded, returning to itself once more. Tents and wagons, metal and cloth and wood and stone and flesh all regained form, though changed into what they *needed* to be, here in this place and time, for the souls of those who would visit. The Carousel lost a level, becoming but a single round of carved horses, the mythological creatures transformed into the mundane. The brightly colored canvas of the main tent faded and dulled, the strands of electric lights disappeared, becoming colored pennants hanging from ropes. The trappings of technology morphed into those of a much simpler era, signs changed to accommodate an alphabet and language different from what they had been. Then the transformation was complete, in less time than it would have taken a human to blink.

The sun rose, and another day began.

He felt people awaken and start the business of their daily lives. Curious, Errante moved to the archway which served as the only entrance and exit to the Carnival — or at least the only one that most people would see. Something felt strange about this place where they'd landed, but his power did not extend far beyond the edge of the tents. He had to actually look with his eyes to see what could be seen and stretch his other senses to their fullest to determine what he could. And when he could see at last, he wished he could not.

"Daniel! Nik! Persephone!" he shouted, his voice loud enough to be heard in every corner of the Carnival. He could hear many running feet coming toward him, yet he could not look away from the terrible sight before him.

"What underworld is this?" A voice spoke beside him, and Errante didn't have to turn his head to know that Nik, the carnival engineer, had arrived. Many others followed in his wake, and there was first silence, then a murmur of voices as people gazed in stunned disbelief at the village before them. Or rather, the remains of what had once been a village, but was now a flattened and burned landscape of twisted, smoking timbers and charred bodies. No tree stood as far as even his eyes could see, and the fabric of time and space was so distorted here that it hid any Paths he might have sensed.

"What cursed destiny brought us to *this* place?" Daniel's

voice came from his other side. The Ringmaster's tone reflected the horror they witnessed, which meant much, given the terrible things he'd endured in his Life Before. Anything that could unsettle a man who had faced down lions and counseled kings was disturbing indeed.

"There is a reason."

This voice was soft and feminine, and Errante forced his gaze away from the carnage to look at Persephone. The Seer appeared shaken, but she held up a card in one hand. On it, a golden wheel was suspended in a blue sky broken by clouds. Arcane symbols were etched in gold on the surface of the wheel, while above it sat a sphinx holding a sword. To one side was a devil-like figure, and to the other, a snake. Of course, there would be a snake.

"Destiny." Errante said softly, and Persephone nodded.

"There is someone here who needs us."

"Well I doubt they'll be coming to find us from there," Daniel pointed out, drawing in a deep breath.

"No." Errante looked around at his people. "Volunteers only. I know it is ugly, but someone here needs help. Who is willing?"

A few people stepped back, a silent refusal, and he didn't feel any judgment toward them for it. But Daniel, Nik, Gentleman Jim, Samson the Strongman, Paul Gallier, Persephone, and several of the roustabouts came forward. They were also joined by Calliope, the tattooed lady. Errante himself could not step from the boundary of the carnival, as they knew, though he hated it when the others walked outside, beyond the ring of his protection. So he watched as they picked their way among the ruins, hoping that none of them became hurt beyond the ability of his magic to heal. No one was ever badly injured or ill where his magic could reach, but not even he, with all his power, could bring someone back from the dead. That Path belonged to another power, and the road between life and death was one that all must Travel alone.

"Carefully," he murmured to himself. "I cannot protect you out there."

Inevitably, they moved from his sight, and he paced back and forth in agitation.

"It is difficult being a parent and watching your children step out where you cannot watch over them, isn't it? I know the feeling well."

Errante turned to find Tia Gallier looking at him with gentle amusement. Yet her green eyes were also full of sympathy, and he took no offense at the comparison. She mothered her brood of flying wonders with loving firmness, yet all her children adored her.

"There is something wrong here," he admitted quietly. He leaned closer, dropping his voice, not wanting any of the roustabouts to hear and to wonder. Tia had been with the Carnival for long enough to know at least some of Errante's powers. "Somehow, there is a hole in the magic. Whatever has befallen this place, it has stripped away the very essence of life. I do not sense the Path of anyone else coming to this place for a long, long time."

Tia's eyes grew wide. "So much damage? But how?"

Errante shook his head. He'd seen places so stripped before, but only when the gods themselves did battle. Yet if that had been the case here, he should have sensed the powers involved, the leftover resonances of fury and hatred. All he felt here was despair, fear, and a grief so profound it made him want to weep.

"You truly do not wish to know," he replied. Whatever had brought them here, he wished to find what they had been sent to seek and be away in case the source of the carnage returned.

It was over an hour, however, measured in linear time,

before Errante saw the small party returning. He was relieved as he sensed each of their unique energies, but he was also puzzled by the blanket-wrapped bundle Calliope held against her shoulder.

They crossed the boundary into the Carnival proper and Errante stepped forward to meet them. "And what have you brought back with you?" he asked.

"Not what, who." Calliope had a tender expression on her face as she moved aside the blanket to show Errante. There, sleeping against her shoulder, was a toddler no older than perhaps two years at most. He couldn't tell if it was a boy or a girl, but the child's dark hair was long and wavy, with thick lashes that curled against rosy cheeks. Strangest of all, the child had no Path Errante could sense; that disturbed him more than anything he'd ever encountered.

Something must have shown on his face because Persephone laid a hand on his arm. "There is no evil — or at least none in the boy," she said softly. "What happened here is another story, but the child is both victim and survivor, not villain. He belongs with us."

"The cards have spoken?" he asked, staring at her. Persephone's magic differed from his own, but it was nearly as powerful. While he read the Path, she recognized the Fate.

"*I* have spoken." She looked at him, one brow arched. "After all this time, do you doubt me?"

"No." He relied upon her judgment too much to question it now. Yet something still disturbed him, something he could sense but not define about this child sleeping so innocently and peacefully in Calliope's arms.

"I'll adopt him as my own, if you will allow it," Calliope said, looking at Errante in appeal. "It has been a long time since I had a child." Every inch of her body except her face was covered in tattoos, and he watched as the patterns on her arms which held the boy shifted and swirled. He caught words as languages emerged and changed, a bit surprised when they at last settled into the ancient tongue of his birth. He saw the name of his own mother, and those of other maternal spirits, along with symbols of protection and love. He did not doubt Calliope's heart, even if his own still held a doubt about the wisdom of this.

"Very well, he may remain," Errante assented at last. Calliope smiled, then turned and headed for her tent, which was striped in tones of sky and sand. The rest of the crew stood nearby, looking to Errante for direction. For a long moment he stood irresolute, but then he mentally shook himself. This was his Carnival. These souls were his family and responsibility. No doubt they had any more desire to remain in this place than he did himself. It grated upon him to be unable to honor the dead, but in reality, there was nothing they could do for the village. Whatever afterlife these people had been destined for, they were in the hands of their gods now.

"Return to your quarters, if you please," he said at last. "It pains me to leave this way, but I do not wish to risk any of you to unknown dangers. We will continue to where our Path next leads us."

He could sense the relief as people drifted away, murmuring among themselves. Finally, he was alone, except for Persephone.

"More advice?" he asked her, smiling crookedly.

"Only one bit more." She looked up at him, eyes bright, and her face shifted as he watched, from young and beautiful to elderly and wise, then back again. "Allow him to grow up. He is a survivor and will be a strong man. I believe he may be as strong as you are. You'll have a need for him, my friend, but as an ally by your side, not a child who requires your protection."

He tilted his head as he regarded her. Sometimes he

wondered what she saw of his Fate, but he never asked — just as she never asked what he himself saw of her Path. They Traveled together, and that was enough. She didn't know everything about his magic, just as he didn't know everything of hers. But she knew well that those who were mortal among them were kept young by his magic. The Galliers, even young Mario, would have long ago been dust but for their place in his family.

"Very well," he agreed.

Persephone smiled. "Excellent. And by the way, his name is Rafael." With that, she turned and headed toward her purple tent.

Errante watched her go, musing on the name. Names had both meaning and power, and Rafael was rich in both. But whether the boy would grow into the name, only time and his Path would tell.

For now, Errante simply waited for everyone to return to their quarters so he could once again put the Carnival to sleep. Only then he would determine where their Path led them next.

CHAPTER 1

"Welcome, Travelers, to the greatest show in the multiverse! Prepare yourself to witness sights that will amaze and delight, intrigue and terrify! Forget all that you think you know about what is possible and give yourself over to the wonders of the Carnival of Mysteries! I'm your Ringmaster, Rafe Harper, and I will tell you of all the amazing acts we've brought to entertain you today!"

Rafe continued his patter as he walked down the Midway, smiling at the patrons who had, as usual, flocked to the Carnival as soon as it had opened. There obviously wasn't as much magic on this world as there was on others they had visited, given the way everyone stared with open mouths and wide eyes at even the simplest of entertainments. It was part of his job to make people feel at ease, using words, his smile, and even the various tricks he knew. Most of it was the simple sleight-of-hand he'd been taught almost as early as he'd learned to walk, but he had some magic of his own. It was minor, especially compared to others in the Carnival, like Persephone or Mephistopheles; it couldn't begin to

9

compete with that of Errante, the owner of the entire thing. Though he'd always known that "owner" was far too simple a word to describe what the Carnival was to Errante.

"Why do you call us travelers?"

Rafe looked down to see a small, solemn faced little girl gazing up at him. She couldn't have been more than six, with brown hair pulled back into a braid and serious hazel eyes. Her clothing was neat and clean, but worn, and of a simple fabric and cut that spoke of an area not blessed with much in the way of wealth. Which didn't matter at all to the Carnival — its purpose wasn't to make money, and more was always given away by the Carnival than was ever taken in.

"Well, aren't you a traveler?" Rafe asked with a smile. "You came here, didn't you?"

"Yes. But it wasn't far." She pointed toward the gate. "Our town is just outside."

"Did you know there are many ways to travel?" He bent his knees, lowering himself down to her level. "It's not just moving from place to place."

"It isn't?" Now she frowned in puzzlement, her forehead creasing in a way Rafe found adorable. She was obviously a deep thinker.

"Oh, no," Rafe replied, lowering his voice confidentially. "We travel through our lives, each day bringing us to a new point in time. We travel in our dreams, our sleeping minds taking us to places we could never go with our feet. We even travel with our hearts, don't we?"

"How can your heart travel?" she asked, eyes widening. "Mine's right here inside me!"

"So it is," he agreed. "But tell me, who do you love most of all in the whole wide world?"

"My mommy." She didn't hesitate at all on the answer. "But she's not here. She had to go to work at the store today. My grandma brought me."

Rafe nodded. "I bet she's a great mother. But tell me, since you love her most, don't you sometimes feel that part of your heart is with her, no matter where she is? And I suspect that a part of her heart is right here with you. That's the best part about love. You can give it and if you're very lucky, you get it back in return. So a bit of your heart travels wherever your mommy goes, and a bit of her heart travels with you."

Thinking of love made Rafe pause, his gaze irresistibly drawn toward the ticket booth, which stood directly across the Midway from the red-and-white striped tent of the Big Top. As usual, Errante stood just inside the boundary of the Carnival proper, watching as the eager attendees queued up to pass beneath the archway. He was dressed in black as he always was, snug fitting breeches tucked into high ebony boots, with a white, full-sleeved shirt beneath a black velvet vest. The outfit emphasized his height and his lean build, while also setting off the olive tone of his skin and the glossy black sheen of his hair. But Errante's eyes were what captivated those who spoke with him, their dark depths holding colors that shifted and swirled and sparked. It often appeared the universe lay within them, vast and endless. Some people, like Rafe, found it fascinating, but others had drawn back in fear. It was like staring into the abyss, only to find the abyss staring back. He'd often thought that what someone saw in Errante's eyes was a reflection of their soul — and any horrors were only of their own creation.

"I like that!" The little girl's words pulled Rafe's attention back to her, and he smiled as he rose back to his full height.

"I do too. It's comforting to know you're never alone, isn't it?" he asked. Then he reached into his pocket and pulled out a special token. "Since you have listened so closely and patiently, this is for you. See? It has a picture of the Carnival on it. You can use this all day to play any game or get anything you want to eat for free. Then you can keep it forever as a reminder of the Carnival."

Her eyes grew wide and round as she accepted the token as though he were handing her the moon. "Grandma, too?"

Chuckling, Rafe nodded. "Grandma too."

She threw her arms around his legs, giving him a hug, then shouted "Thank you!" as she ran off into the crowds, no doubt to find her grandmother and share the news. Rafe watched her go, knowing she was safe — no harm befell anyone in the Carnival because Errante wouldn't allow it. And no child who entered ever left hungry or sad unless their Fate decreed it must be so.

When he glanced toward the entrance again, Errante had disappeared, as he often did, drawn away by something that required his specific attention or magic. As he started back along the Midway, continuing his advertising for the shows and rides, Rafe wondered what Errante saw when he looked at all the people flowing past him. Errante's magic moved the carnival from world to world, across time and space. It changed the form of everything around them to fit into the places they went, making them blend in rather than stand out. It enabled the members of the Carnival to understand any language spoken to them, and allowed them to be understood in return, an effect which lingered even if they stepped beyond the boundary of the Carnival proper and went out to explore whatever world they were on. Errante only said that they were to be careful outside the confines of his magic, since he himself never left the perimeter. Within the Carnival, no one was ever hurt badly, no one ever became sick or died — and that included the patrons who visited. It was only outside the invisible boundary of Errante's magic that life continued as normal. The Carnies themselves didn't even age — except, that was, for Rafe himself. Brought into the Carnival as a toddler too young to remember where he'd come from or who his parents had been, he'd been allowed to grow up. He'd spent his childhood happily running around the Carnival, learning bits and pieces of things from the acts and the roustabouts, becoming familiar with every aspect and corner of what was his home. For a while Mario Gallier, youngest son of the aerialists, had been his companion in age, but then Rafe had grown up, while Mario happily remained a boy.

Calliope, his foster mother, had also made sure he was educated, and she had books about every subject in the multiverse, which he'd easily absorbed like an eager sponge, learning much about the universe they traveled and the worlds within it. Then when Daniel, the former Ringmaster, had asked to return to the Kingdom from which he'd originally come, Errante had approached a by-then young adult Rafael and offered him the position of Ringmaster. He'd also offered the flip side of the coin — Rafael could leave the Carnival at any time or place he chose, with resources to do whatever he desired. But by that point Rafe had been as much in love with Errante as the Carnival, and he wasn't about to leave. He'd accepted the offer, and he had been wearing the top hat and the fancy red coat with its flashy buttons and trim ever since.

Somewhere around his thirtieth year, he, too, had stopped aging. He had to be at least seventy by now, he figured, but his skin was still firm and smooth, his eyesight and hearing were keen as ever, and no gray was to be found in the inky blackness of his hair.

As far as how old Errante was… well, even Persephone couldn't venture a guess. Or, if she had, she refused to share her knowledge with anyone. She, too, was far, far older than she appeared, and she kept her secrets well.

Errante was, as the saying went, a mystery inside an enigma, wrapped in a conundrum so deep that no light seemed to penetrate its depths. He was kind, and he did much for people on worlds who didn't even realize they were being assisted, all with no desire for repayment or recognition. He was also the most fascinating and attractive man Rafe had seen on any world across the thousands he had visited — and the one man Rafe knew he couldn't have, no matter how much he might want him.

It was unfortunate that Errante seemed to be so separate from everyone around him, even the members of his "family", as he called those belonging to the Carnival. Even Persephone, who could read a person's Fate with unfailing accuracy, would only say of Errante that "he's the loneliest man I've ever known."

Lonely he might be, but he was also kind and generous, and fiercely protective of those within the Carnival, whether it was someone who'd been with him for centuries, like Persephone, or the newest roustabout who might stay only a day or two before moving on. And each person who left the Carnival did so richer for having worked there, never hopeless or defeated as they may have entered it. Rafe himself was also grateful to Errante, because Calliope had never hidden from him the circumstances under which Rafe had come into her care. She had loved him as fiercely as though he had been flesh of her flesh, and Rafe loved her just as much in return. But she always insisted firmly that it had been Errante who had truly saved him from a death that would likely have been lonely and lingering.

"She is special."

The voice came from close to his right side, but Rafe wasn't even startled. He turned his head, unsurprised to find Errante next to him. For a moment he wondered if Errante had been reading his thoughts about Calliope, but then he followed the direction of Errante's gaze, catching sight of the little girl again. She was pulling a gray-haired woman along by the hand, the token clutched in her small fist as she made her way with determination toward the ice cream vendor.

"Oh?" Rafe asked.

"Indeed." Errante smiled slightly, the corners of his eyes crinkling, although no wrinkles would remain when the expression faded. "You will see her again. Her Path and ours will cross once more when the time is right. She has magic she has not yet felt, but she will before long. Persephone will be a good tutor."

"As Calliope was for me?"

Rafe didn't know why he'd said the words, or why they came out so sharply. He regretted them immediately, wondering if Errante would feel he was ungrateful. But Errante only inclined his head in acknowledgement, some expression Rafe couldn't interpret crossing his face before swiftly disappearing.

"She loved you as her own." Errante's voice was deep and melodious, and full of certainty. "She taught you well, but she was your mother, first and always."

"She was. I'm sorry." Rafe didn't want Errante to think he was ungrateful.

"I am not offended." Errante shrugged slightly. "Just remember that Calliope wanted you from the moment she first saw you, and whatever Fate was involved in our finding you, it was so that she could be your mother, no matter what else happened. She cherished you for no other reason than love."

Rafe wanted so badly to ask, "And you — could you ever love me?" The words were there on his tongue, almost burning him with the desire to say them. But he couldn't, and so only smiled instead.

"Well, I'm glad to know I'll see our young friend again one day. She is special."

Errante nodded, then turned more businesslike. "I will

leave you to your duties. We shall move on tonight. The moon shines, and our business here is done." With that, he moved away, but as he turned, Rafe was certain he heard the familiar deep voice add, "Never forget you are special as well." But perhaps that was only wishful thinking on his part.

Shaking himself, he moved back along the Midway. They would leave tonight, but for today, he had a job to do. His life would probably be considered strange to the people who walked past him, awed by sights and sounds and smells of a place that to them was magical, although how *truly* magical they would never know. But it was his life, and he loved it, and there wasn't anywhere else he'd rather be — other than in Errante's arms.

"Hurry, ladies and gentlemen, the Big Top show featuring the Flying Galliers is starting in ten minutes! Seats are going fast, so don't be left out of a once in a lifetime opportunity to see this family of daredevil acrobats defying gravity and performing feats that will leave your jaws on the floor! Their show is even more awe-inspiring when you see they perform without a net! Come one, come all, and see the most breath-taking show in the Carnival of Mysteries!"

CHAPTER 2

Standing near the entrance to the Big Top, Errante listened to the music of the calliope and watched Rafe work the crowd. He made the consummate Ringmaster, with a booming voice and a manner that could charm even the most jaded visitor into a smile. His dark hair was thick and glossy, his brown eyes bright and full of happiness. His broad shoulders, emphasized by his ornately trimmed red coat, attracted far more admiring eyes than just Errante's. And if sometimes, in the darkness of his room, Errante dreamed of how that strong, muscular body might feel against his, well, he probably wasn't alone in that regard either. Rafe was an extremely attractive man, and Errante wasn't blind.

Watching Rafe in action was something he had found himself doing more often than he should in the last forty years or so, but he couldn't help it. There was something about Rafe that always drew his attention, no matter where in the Carnival he was or what he was doing. Errante tried to tell himself it was simply the same interest he took in any of the long-time residents of the Carnival, his family of choice, but deep down where he kept his most private thoughts, he knew it wasn't true.

Rafe drew him in a way no one ever had in his long, long life. And made him yearn for something he could never have.

He supposed it wasn't too odd, given the role propinquity often played in human feelings. And for all his great power and age, Errante did have feelings, buried as he kept them most of the time. But Errante had maintained his distance from Rafe for the first two decades after Calliope brought him into the Carnival. At first it was from suspicion, because the fact remained that Rafe had been discovered in very unusual circumstances, and Errante knew his great enemy would use any method at his disposal, even a young child, to bring about Errante's downfall. Added to that was the fact that while he could see the Path of almost every living being, he could not see Rafael's.

It was Errante's gift to see where people would Travel. It wasn't simply knowing of their movements across time and space, but where they *needed* to be. The Path that had led them to the world where Rafe had been discovered had not been Rafe's, but Calliope's — just as her Path had led her out of the Carnival some time later, and would, someday, lead her back once more. At first, Errante had thought that Rafe was just too young to have developed a Path of his own, in the way children were often difficult to separate from their parents. Calliope's Path to Rafe had been so strong, it might have overshadowed the child's, or perhaps even have merged with it to make the draw as powerful as what Errante had seen. There was also the horrific place where Rafe had been discovered — something of the energies which had caused that level of devastation could have muddled the magic Errante usually tracked. So he had waited, always staying on the periphery of the boy's life as he had grown, watching to see when his Path would indicate his purpose and time to leave the Carnival.

Only it had never happened, which was both disturbing and yet strangely intriguing. And his fascination with Rafe had grown and changed as the boy became a man.

For a time Errante had considered summarily banishing Rafe from the Carnival when he reached adulthood, or even sending him off with Calliope when her own Path had called her elsewhere. Each time, something had stopped him, some instinct that told him it wasn't yet time. Or maybe it was simply Persephone's words from that day so long ago, echoing within him: he would have need of Rafe someday. Then when Daniel had finally tired of the wandering life and asked Errante to take him home, Errante had been faced with a dilemma — he needed a Ringmaster, yet no one suitable was available. No one, that was, except Rafe.

It had taken Errante a few days of inner turmoil before he had approached Rafe with the offer — to become Ringmaster, or to find his fortune away from the Carnival. He had been strangely relieved when Rafe had stayed, but, even at that point, he still wasn't certain what the future might hold. He only knew that a bond had been growing slowly between them, so that Rafe was now more important to him than anyone else had ever been. It disturbed and worried him, but it also made his ancient heart beat faster whenever Rafe was near.

He caught sight of two men by the carousel and set aside his ruminations. He, too, had a job to do in the Carnival, and it was time he was about it.

The pair by the carousel seemed to be enjoying the sight, and Errante smiled to himself. People from worlds where magic wasn't common — or where it was distrusted, as it was on this one — rarely believed what was right before their eyes. The animals all acknowledged Errante's presence as he stood there, while the people blinked in astonishment, unwilling to believe they'd seen the figures they considered but constructs of wood and paint move. But one of the two men seemed unfazed, no doubt because his aura fairly glowed with magic of his own. The Paths of these two intertwined, but they faced several problems, which is no doubt what led them to the Carnival.

He came up behind them. "Beautiful, isn't it?"

The taller man jumped, startled, as he turned. He looked Errante up and down before obviously deciding he wasn't a threat. "It's the most amazing carousel I've ever seen. Who's the artist?"

Now that was a question indeed, given that Imhotep had perished some forty-seven centuries before either of these men had drawn breath. "No one you would know, and long gone. But thank you for caring to ask." People in modern times, Errante had found, rarely had much care for the artistry in things they considered mere amusements. No doubt they would be even more shocked to learn that a man named Da Vinci had painted the portrait banners of the acts which hung along the Midway.

Unsurprisingly, the mage was less impressed and obviously suspicious. "Who are you?"

"I am Errante Ame, and this is my Carnival," he replied. He teased the mage a bit. "Our show is full of wonders and delights that will leave you breathless, but whether that is with amazement or dread depends entirely upon you." He glanced at the taller man, then back at the mage, who continued to stare back with stoicism. A hard sell, but if Errante was to help them along their Path, he would need to believe.

At that moment, a small, beautifully colored conure swept down from the Carousel and landed on the mage's shoulder.

Errante nodded a greeting to the familiar, who nodded back, and spoke. "Traveler."

Errante smiled widely, pleased to recognize a fellow Traveler. There was an energy that surrounded all beings who crossed the multiverse, and the familiar recognized it in Errante, even as Errante recognized it in him. The familiar was old and wise, and would see to it that the mage did what was needed. "I see you are people of goodwill. Have no fear. Let us entertain you, perhaps find you something to aid in your quest. For time and worlds are fleeting, but each soul has a tale to tell."

He turned then, and headed off into the crowd, greeting other visitors who seemed enchanted by the Carousel. When he reached the edge of the Midway, he turned again at the sound of Rafe's booming voice announcing the next show for the Galliers. Rafe was clearly in his element, and Errante took a moment to admire the sight of him. Even if he could never touch, he could always look his fill.

"He's grown into quite a confident, handsome man, hasn't he?"

Persephone spoke up from beside him, and Errante looked down at her, one brow raised at the inane observation. She was as capable of approaching unseen as he was himself, so it was never surprising for her to turn up, especially when he was alone. Yet her words drew his attention, as Persephone rarely said anything that didn't have a deeper meaning.

"He has been a grown man for decades," he replied. "You are just noticing this now?"

"Of course not." She reached out to smack him lightly on the arm, a chastising gesture. "Nor are *you* only noticing it now."

He stiffened. "I have no idea what you mean." If he had been so obvious that others had noticed, it might be time for him to tell Rafe to go, as little as he wanted to do it. If Persephone had noticed, others would, and if the wrong one did, Rafe's life would be over before it had really begun.

She rolled her eyes. "Don't try that with me, you old fraud," she said, dropping her voice. They were well separated from other people, but Persephone respected privacy. "I'm almost as old as you are, and I've watched *you* watching *him* long enough to have an idea where your heart lies."

The thought he'd revealed himself shook him, even if he trusted Persephone as he trusted few others. He decided to break their unspoken agreement. "So is that what you have Seen?" he asked.

"I can't *see* your Fate with clarity, as you well know," she retorted. "Shadows of possibilities at the best, which is what I have seen since he first arrived. You need him, and as the man he's become, not the boy he was. I can see but little more of his Fate, if I'm honest." She shrugged. "It's that way, sometimes. Either there is something obscuring my vision, or there are simply too many possibilities. Or the person I'm trying to See is more powerful than myself and blocking my vision."

He heard the tartness in her tone, and it made him smile despite the seriousness of the topic. More than perhaps anyone but Nik, who was attuned to the energies of the multiverse in a way far different from any Errante had encountered before, Persephone was aware of just how much magic Errante had poured into the Carnival over the years. It was encased in a protective cocoon deeper than the oceans of old Earth, harder and stronger than diamond. The Carnival could withstand even the heart of a sun or the cold of the abyss, and those within its boundaries would be safe. It was what Errante needed in order to feel safe himself.

"Not intentionally, you know." He smiled again. "After so long, hiding becomes a habit, I suppose."

"If you have any sense, you'll stop hiding from happiness." She squeezed his arm in sympathy. "Even the Gods themselves had mates."

And I know how well that turned out in the end, he thought darkly.

Persephone must have seen something in his eyes, for her own grew wide. "Errante… I'm sorry. I wasn't trying to upset you."

"I know." He drew in a deep breath. "Just trust that I know what I am doing, if you can." He'd long ago told Persephone that someone pursued him, though he didn't tell her who — or even who he himself truly was. Not because he didn't trust her, but because it was safer for her to know only what was necessary. He needed her help, and she had agreed to let him know if she ever had a vision of something dark and evil approaching. She'd been with him for a very long time, and so far he'd avoided the danger that haunted his every move.

"I always have," she replied simply.

Errante nodded, letting the subject drop. "There will be a mage coming to see you later on. He and his lover have an interesting problem and will need your guidance."

"I'll see to it." She smiled at him, and then, in a swirl of skirts, she set off behind the tents back toward her own.

With a final, unconsciously longing glance at Rafe, Errante set off toward the closest gaming area. There was a certain witch doll there with a role to play, and he needed to see to it that its ruby slippers fell into the right hands.

LATER THAT NIGHT, when all was quiet, Errante moved the Carnival. As he stepped through the vastness of the multiverse, he noticed an infinitesimally small area wreathed in darkness from which no light escaped and to which no Paths led. Pausing, he stared at it — had its future somehow been erased? Had something he himself had done closed off that area to him? But perhaps it had always been that way, and he'd never noticed before. The cosmos he crossed was vast, and he usually had his vision turned toward the Path he followed. Yet it still made him uneasy, and for now he had to Travel where he was needed.

Pushing it into the back of his mind, he took another step, settling down on the ground of yet another world. Around him, the Carnival once again began its metamorphosis.

Another day was about to begin.

CHAPTER 3

"**I** like this place," Simeon said, gazing around the town square. "Reminds me a bit of home, yeah?"

Rafe looked around as well, pleased to find several pubs lining the sides of the open area, already doing a brisk business despite the early hour. Not that time of day mattered much to either him or Simeon, given that sleep in the Carnival was always restful. And when Errante declared an "off day", everyone was usually eager to take advantage of the opportunity to see what the world they were visiting offered. Though in the last few years, Rafe had often chosen to remain in the Carnival, popping out usually just long enough to find a place selling books, if such a thing existed close by, or watching whatever visual media was on offer on the more technologically advanced worlds. The screens in everyone's quarters always altered to whatever would be the standard for where they'd ended up, though they often disappeared altogether, replaced by mirrors or artwork. He didn't mind that, but he was often perturbed when his en suite toilet — one perk of being Ringmaster — was replaced by a bowl and pitcher with a chamber pot. He'd often wondered if he could coerce Errante into somehow retaining "modern conveniences," at least in the private bathrooms.

"Is it the number of pubs or the fog?" he teased Simeon. The cheerful roustabout — who didn't look too much younger than Rafe — grinned up at him.

"Both," Simeon laughed. "And I'll enjoy them while I can."

"Just be careful here with your charming words and taking ways," Rafe said, mock-seriously. "Errante can't do much about the local coppers if you find yourself just too tempted to hold back. Though I suppose I could always tell them you're my little brother that our mum dropped on his head, so you didn't know what you were doing." In reality, with his long dark hair and jet eyes, Simeon looked enough like Rafe that it was plausible. The similarity of their durable clothing, which usually was of the sort that placed them in the "middle class" of wherever they were, also contributed to the resemblance.

"Don't worry about me, mate," Simeon replied cheekily. "Want to crawl the pubs? I'm fancying a pint, and I hope I can find one that tastes as good as the ones in the carnival."

They'd walked together over to the small town from where the carnival had set up nearby. Rafe looked back toward where they'd left it, but of course nothing was visible through the fog. Not that it had been foggy *inside* the Carnival, but magic seemed at a low ebb in this place, no doubt one reason beyond simple kindness that Errante had closed for the day. It was never a good idea for the Carnival to stand out as too odd.

"Nah, you go on without me. I saw a bunch of the other roustabouts head out earlier. I bet you can find them easily enough. I'll catch up later. I'm going to see if I can find a bookseller."

Simeon raised a brow at him, then shrugged. "Have fun then. And don't do anything I wouldn't."

Rafe chuckled. "What wouldn't you do?" he asked, then watched as Simeon gave him an impudent grin and set off toward one of the brightly lit pubs.

There weren't many people out in the square, so Rafe headed toward the side opposite of where Simeon had gone, checking out the shops. The technology in this place was low level, with electric lights but lacking motorized vehicles. His shoes were silent on the cobbled streets, and he smelled the distinctive scents of hay and horse dung as he passed an alley. The storefronts were ones he'd seen plenty of times in many different places: dressmakers, milliners, a flower seller whose tempting scents were muted in the dampness. The fog swirled around him, growing thicker, hiding the other side of the square. He passed a pub, hearing piano music and voices inside, mixed with the clinking of glassware and cutlery. The curtains were open, and he watched the people as he strolled past, some chatting with others, a few sitting alone in silence. A snapshot of life in a place he might never see again.

He was about to give up and move along to the next side of the square, when at the corner he passed a set of dark windows. In gold lettering it declared "Fell's Books", and Rafe smiled in pleasure. Some places that seemed civilized on the surface hadn't learned to treasure the printed word, and he was relieved this wasn't one of them.

A set of simple wooden steps led up to the door, and as he stepped inside, a bell rang merrily overhead. He paused for a moment to breathe in the familiar scents of paper and leather, taking in the bookshelves literally everywhere in the shop, and a desk off to one side where the only other occupant of the place was seated.

A pleasant faced, rather plump man with blond ringlets, dressed in a waistcoat and jacket, looked up as he entered. He gave Rafe a wide smile as he put down his teacup and stood.

"Good morning! I'm Fell, welcome to my shop. Is there anything I can help you find today?"

"Good morning," Rafe replied. He gestured to all the books. "I'm really just browsing. I read quite a lot, and I'm always looking for something I've not read before."

"Ah, a fellow bibliophile. That's splendid!" Fell rubbed his hands together, his eyes shining with eagerness. It seemed a little odd to Rafe, whose normal experience of booksellers had shown they were more absent minded or withdrawn, but it was interesting to encounter someone different after all this time. "What will you have? Fiction? There is an interesting work by a fellow named Darwin that was published rather recently. I assume you've already done the classics. Perhaps history?" Fell paused in his stream of conscious rambling and peered at Rafe closely. Then his blue eyes widened, and he shook his head. "No, no history. You, my good man, are obviously a man for mythology. Follow me."

Rafe blinked, then obediently followed in Fell's wake as he slipped his way with surprising dexterity through books piled on chairs, on tables, and perched precariously on the tops of sturdy shelving units that nevertheless seemed in danger of collapse from the weight. He finally stopped in front of a set of shelves that were covered with glass doors.

"These are special, but I think you're just the man who will appreciate the care and research that went into these tomes."

Fell opened one door, then reached in and selected a book. Turning, he held it out to Rafe. "Yes, this one is perfect for you."

Rafe reached out to take the book, and as he did, he could *feel* the magic that was reaching him from Fell, transmitted through the book. He stared, wondering if Fell was a mage in hiding on this world, and, if so, if his purpose was benign or malign. But looking into Fell's guileless eyes, he somehow instinctively felt the good in the man.

In a way, Fell somehow reminded him of Errante, or Persephone, though he wasn't certain if it was age, or the sense of deep knowledge. But Rafe's instincts weren't warning him of anything sinister, as they occasionally had in the past.

Fell released the book, and the moment passed. Rafe looked down at the front, seeing the title embossed in gold leaf. "The Myths and Legends of Ancient Egypt," he read aloud. What was an Egypt? Was it a person, or a place he'd never heard of?

"This is simply the latest information," Fell said, motioning Rafe back toward the front of the shop. "A friend of mine has been heavily involved in the digs, and he had a lot of input on this book. Thank goodness for the Rosetta Stone — otherwise all those hieroglyphs would still be a puzzle, right?"

"Right," Rafe agreed, though he wasn't entirely certain what the mage was talking about. Had a magic stone somehow helped them translate? Not that he could let his ignorance show, since apparently Fell considered him well-read enough to understand the reference.

Still bemused, he followed Fell, then handed over the book again so that Fell could wrap it up in paper, then add a piece of oilskin over that, before tying it up securely with string. "There we are. That'll be five florins, please."

Rafe reached into his pocket and removed the version of a wallet that had materialized on his dresser this morning. The money inside had changed as well, but he counted out five of the bills and passed them to Fell.

"I hope you have a good day, and enjoy the book," Fell said.

"Thank you, I'm sure I will," Rafe replied.

A few moments later he found himself outside the shop, feeling a bit mystified about what had happened. It had been an odd encounter, but given that Rafe's entire life had been comprised of odd encounters, perhaps this one hadn't been very special after all.

Shaking his head, he tucked the well-wrapped book under his arm, then continued on around the square. He passed several more shops, a hotel, and even a smithy, smelling of hot iron and ringing with the blows of metal on metal. Finally, he reached the opposite side from the bookstore, where there was a pub with a sign declaring it "The Sacred Band."

His eyes widened, though he wasn't sure if the term had the same meaning in this world as it had on a few others, but he decided it was a good place to stop for a pint and a bite.

The interior was warm and dim, but it smelled invitingly of beer and something savory. As he looked around, he spotted Simeon at the bar with a couple of the other roustabouts, so he went over to join them.

"How's the beer?" he asked, sliding onto a stool next to Simeon and laying the book on the bar.

"S'great!" Simeon replied with a grin. He signaled to the barman. "A pint for my mate, if you please! And one of the pork pies." He looked at Rafe smugly. "You can thank me later."

The food and drink appeared quickly. The other roustabouts, two of a set of triplets, raised their glasses as Rafe took a drink. "Oh my, that *is* good!"

"Just like home," Simeon said with contentment. There were the remnants of a pork pie on a plate in front of him as well, reduced to little more than crumbs. "We eat well at the carnival, yeah, but this is like home."

"Your accent even fits right in," Rafe said, lowering his voice.

"That it does," Simeon agreed. Then he grew serious. "Not that I'm thinking of staying behind, mind. The carnival is the best job I've ever had. Not looking to give it up yet."

"No need to, not until you're ready," Rafe replied. Then he bit into the pork pie, which was hot and savory and delicious. As Simeon had said, the food in the carnival was excellent, but it was nice to have something different now and then.

They chatted about other meals they'd had, especially Bill and Bob, who had been part of another show and had traveled widely. Rafe finished the pork pie, then sighed. As much as he loved his job, sometimes it really was nice to get away for a little while and see something different. He wondered if Errante ever regretted the fact that he couldn't step beyond the edge of the carnival. Rafe wasn't certain if he was voluntarily tied to it or not, but whichever it was, he imagined even something as wonderful and special might pall after centuries.

Then Simeon leaned closer, dropping his voice. "Look out, you've got an admirer."

Simeon was looking down the bar past Rafe, and Rafe turned his head. A man, tall, broad, and red-haired, was looking at him with a hungry smile. He was attractive, but while Rafe was no stranger to sex, the man simply wasn't his type. He favored tall, slender, dark-haired men, which he knew hadn't been lost on Calliope over the years, even if she'd said nothing about it. But he was now curious about why the man was so blatant, so he glanced around the rest of the bar, noticing for the first time that the clientele was exclusively male, and a few of the patrons were sitting rather close together.

"Ah, so the name wasn't false advertising," he said quietly, and when Simeon raised a brow, he went on. "The Sacred Band of Thebes was a military unit made up entirely of gay men. They beat the shit out of the Spartans, at least on what Calliope, my adoptive mother, called 'Old Earth'. I'd wondered when I saw the name if it meant the same here, and apparently it does."

"Interesting," Simeon replied. "Having gotten my arse kicked for my preferences a few times, I'm glad to know our side sometimes did the kicking." He paused. "You should go for it, if you want to. He looks as if he'd like to eat you up like one of the pork pies."

Rafe chuckled and shook his head. "Not this time, but thanks for the encouragement. I've got a new book from an odd little bookshop, so I think I'll head back and see if it's as interesting as the proprietor indicated." He rose to his feet, taking out his wallet and putting enough money, according to the menu on the board, to pay for his food, plus that of the others. "Enjoy yourselves, boys, but don't get into too much trouble. I'll be annoyed if I have to come back and bail any of you out."

The roustabouts laughed as Rafe picked up his book and walked toward the front. The redhead watched after him, but Rafe only nodded politely to him, then headed out the door.

Outside, the fog had thickened even more. It was a little disconcerting, but Rafe knew where the carnival was, so he headed off in that direction. In the way of fog, sounds had become muted and difficult to track, but he thought he could faintly hear the music of the calliope.

"Where are you going in such a rush, then?"

Rafe stopped, turning around to find the red-head from the pub a few feet behind him.

"Back where I belong," Rafe replied. He didn't like the way the man was looking at him. Not that he was worried. They were of a similar height, but while the red-head was broader in the shoulders, Rafe was strong. If the guy was looking to rob him or fight him, Rafe felt he could hold his own. But he'd prefer to avoid a confrontation if possible. Carnies mixing it up with the locals could create difficulties he'd rather avoid.

"Not very friendly, are you?" The man stepped closer, but Rafe held his ground.

"I'm quite friendly. It's part of my job," Rafe said, keeping his voice even. "But I'm off duty now, so I'd just as soon be going."

"You're with that carnival. I recognize the type." There was a sneer in the man's voice now, and his expression grew harsh. "Wandering around, vagabonds, rootless and shiftless, but still thinking you're too good for the likes of us locals, right? Come into town, empty our pockets, then be gone without consequences."

"Not at all." Rafe drew himself up to his full height. He was proud of his job, of his life, of the good that the carnival did for people, even if they didn't know it. They *helped* people, they didn't take advantage of them. "I'm not sure where your anger comes from, but it's misdirected. Our carnival has harmed no one nor any place we've been. I've been Ringmaster for... a long time, and we've never had a complaint."

"A likely story," the man said derisively. "Well, I think you should be taught a lesson about respecting your betters. I won't have some piece of carnie trash acting like he's too good for me!"

From the man's expression, he was determined to turn this into a confrontation, no matter what Rafe said or did. He only had one more thing to try, as little as he wanted to do it. He hated giving in to bullies, but really, it was for the man's own protection. While Errante's magic couldn't protect Rafe out here, there was no telling what people like Samson or Mephistopheles, who were good friends of his, might do in retaliation. "Look, you think we've taken from your town, maybe from you? Why don't I give you all the money I have? Would that make you feel it's more fair?"

"You trying to buy me off?" the man laughed nastily. "Should have known you were a coward as well as a thief."

Rafe shook his head and sighed. "I was trying to protect *you*, you idiot. You're messing with things far beyond your understanding."

Apparently the man didn't appreciate being called an idiot, because he made a strangled sound of fury and rushed at Rafe. But Rafe had trained with the Galliers from the time he could walk, so he easily somersaulted over the man's head.

"What the fuck?" The red-head whirled, staring at Rafe, obviously surprised to find Rafe standing a few feet away and looking back at him calmly. "What stupid trick is that? I'm going to break you into pieces!"

"Are you?" Rafe's adrenaline was flowing. He didn't like to fight, although he had sparred with Samson and some of the roustabouts many times for fun. He'd not gotten into a disagreement with a local in probably fifty years, when he'd been young and dumb and a little too full of himself.

Another incoherent sound preceded the man rushing at him again. But apparently the red-head was an experienced fighter, since he now watched how Rafe was moving more carefully. He actually got a hand on the plain brown coat Rafe was wearing, but Rafe twisted, slipping out of the garment, though he had to drop the book he was holding to do it.

The red-head tossed down the coat, then rushed at Rafe again. Rafe stepped to one side and smacked the man on the back of the head as he passed.

"Son of a bitch, I'm going to kill you!" the man spat, then there was a flash as he pulled a knife from one pocket of his pants.

The equation had suddenly changed a bit, but Rafe kept

his eyes on the knife, as Gentleman Jim had taught him. It wasn't a long blade, but a strike in the right place could disable Rafe, or even kill him. It was a good thing Errante had stressed to them all many times that he couldn't save them outside the Carnival. Otherwise, he might have done something rash.

The man lunged again, and Rafe sprang back. He chopped at the man's wrist, and the solid contact jarred his entire arm. But it also made the guy drop the knife, and Rafe knew he was going to have to take his chance to knock the man out.

Another somersault surprised the guy enough to let Rafe get behind him. He hooked one arm around the red-head's neck, intending to squeeze just enough to knock him unconscious. It would leave him with a bitch of a headache, but it was better than Rafe breaking his neck, as he easily could.

The man flailed, one hand grasping at Rafe's arm that was holding him fast. But what Rafe didn't see, and didn't realize until an intense pain shot through his stomach, was that the red-head apparently had another knife.

The agonizing sensation of several inches of metal being thrust into his gut almost brought Rafe to his knees. But he held on, an anger stronger than any he could ever remember feeling burning along every nerve of his body. This man, this *bastard*, had hunted him down, insulted him, insulted the carnival, then threatened him, and all Rafe had done was to try to leave in peace. Now he'd been stabbed, and he was furious that he might be dying, and he'd never get to tell Errante how he felt.

He felt himself growing warm, then hot, and his vision went white. He was burning all over, and he moved his arm, letting the red-head fall at his feet, not caring about his attacker at this point.

Is this what dying feels like? He wondered, dropping to his knees. *Like I'm burning up?*

He didn't know how long he knelt there, but slowly his vision cleared a bit. He could see his hands, which looked like they were glowing, but that wasn't possible. He shook his head, reaching down to press against the stab wound, hoping he could staunch the blood long enough to get back to the carnival.

But his fingers encountered nothing, and for a moment he was confused. He pressed harder, and then he felt skin. Smooth, unbroken skin.

A breath of surprise passed his lips, and suddenly his vision cleared completely. He was still kneeling on the cobblestones, which were rough against the skin of his legs. He looked down, shocked to find that he was completely naked. There was no sign at all of his clothing or his shoes.

Or of his wound.

Confused, he thumped down on his ass, surprised that the stones against his bare butt were warm and dry. His attacker was sprawled awkwardly next to him, out cold. The skin of his attacker's neck was reddened, and the fabric of his coat and shirt were singed.

"What in the hell?" Rafe couldn't wrap his mind around what had happened. But his attacker began to stir, and that spurred him into action. His abandoned coat was only a couple of feet away, so he snatched it up and donned it. He wished he had time to strip his attacker of his shoes and pants, but from the way the man was moaning, he was quickly regaining consciousness. Rafe scooped up the book, and then turned, looking around, having lost his bearings during the fight. Which way was home?

Then he heard it again — the cheerful tones of the calliope, from its home in the middle of the carousel. He'd recognize Kal's playing anywhere, but which way was it coming from? The fog muted and misdirected, and he turned in place, seeking the music.

Some sense urged him in one direction, so he went, listening intently for the notes that beckoned him. Behind him, he heard his attacker bellow, either in anger or pain, but Rafe didn't care. He continued forward, hoping that the redhead couldn't follow him. He needed to get away.

The music grew louder, and Rafe almost cried out in relief. He clenched his jaw, moving as quickly as he could, the strains of some unique composition of Kal's strengthening his steps until he was almost running.

Then the fog thinned, and lights appeared, haloed and faint at first, but growing brighter every moment. A few steps further and he could differentiate their colors, as they twinkled merrily as though in time to the music. The fog swirled, and the familiar arch came into sight. Another few steps, and he passed the magical boundary that defined the Carnival of Mysteries.

For once, Errante wasn't standing in wait behind the ticket booth, for which Rafe was grateful. In fact, no one at all seemed to be around. He couldn't even see Kal, hidden as he was behind the carousel, intent on his practice. But the music Kal played would be engraved in Rafe's mind and heart forever, the melody that had beckoned him like magic back to his home.

Tired and confused, Rafe kept to the side of the Midway, making his way back to his private quarters. He didn't even bother to remove the coat, crossing the room in a few steps and dropping face down into the soft, warm surface of his familiar bed. He never felt the book drop from his fingers, as darkness enveloped him, driving out fear and confusion in sleep's comforting embrace.

CHAPTER 4

Something was wrong.

Errante watched with concern as Rafe went about his job. Perhaps others didn't notice the lack of spring in his step, how his smile didn't reach his dark eyes, or the mechanical tone of his booming voice, but Errante certainly did. It concerned and puzzled him, and left him wondering what he should do about it.

It had started only a short time before, just after Errante had given the Carnival a day off. Something must have happened on that world, but he couldn't imagine what it could be. An altercation with a fellow Traveler, perhaps? Or something else, perhaps leaving behind a lover?

The thought gave Errante a pang, which he didn't like. Not that he was angry at Rafe, not at all. He was annoyed with himself for feeling a jealousy which was totally unfounded. Rafe was young and handsome, and he deserved a partner. Just because Errante, deep down, wished to *be* that partner didn't give him a right to begrudge Rafe's happiness.

He considered asking Persephone to approach Rafe. The Seer was easy to talk to, as Errante well knew, and she could counsel Rafe on whatever was disturbing him. Yet he knew Persephone well enough to know exactly what she would tell him if Errante made that request — *talk to him yourself*. And she would be right to do so.

Following him along the Midway, Errante waited until Rafe took a short break and stepped behind a tent, away from the crowds of laughing people. Rafe stood, head down, shoulders sagging, and Errante ached for the way the pose spoke so eloquently of despair. He stepped up behind Rafe and laid a hand on his shoulder. He couldn't help but feel the warmth of Rafe's body through his Ringmaster's coat, and the tingle of magic that flowed between them.

Rafe's head snapped up, and he turned sharply, knocking Errante's hand away and taking a step back, almost tripping over a spike anchoring the tent to the ground. Shocked, Errante stepped back as well, stunned by both the reaction and the fear he easily read in Rafe's dark eyes.

The expression was quickly erased by surprise and horror, and Rafe moved toward Errante, holding up a hand in appeal. "I'm sorry! I... you surprised me. I didn't realize it was you."

Errante inclined his head in acceptance of the explanation, but he was more concerned than ever. "If you will pardon my intrusion, Rafael, I cannot help but notice that something is disturbing you." He smiled, trying to be reassuring, because Rafe's confusion and fear tore at Errante's heart. "Do you need to speak to someone? I am considered a good listener, but if you are uncomfortable with me, perhaps Persephone? Or Tia Gallier?"

Rafe bit his lip, hesitating, but then he nodded. "Yes, I... I think I need to tell someone what happened. If only to keep myself from thinking I'm losing my mind." He ran a hand through his hair. For all that Rafe had already lived more years than most mortals did, he seemed young and vulnerable now.

"Come, then." Errante led the way behind the tent, where a path allowed performers and roustabouts to move without being seen. One end of it led toward Persephone's tent at the end of the midway, and the other to the group of trailers, caravans, and RVs that made up housing for the carnival members. Errante had a trailer of his own, set a short distance from the others, which served as his personal space and office. Rafe quietly followed along behind him.

They stepped inside, the interior cool and dim after the bright sunlight of the day. The front area contained a desk and several chairs — not that Errante had any need of a desk as such, but he'd found that many people who needed to discuss things with him felt reassured by its presence. But he moved past that area, into his quarters, and motioned for Rafe to have a seat on one of the comfortable chairs arranged around the room. He sometimes entertained part of the crew on their off days, so Rafe had been here often, if never for this reason.

Rafe chose a seat, and Errante took one across from him, close enough so they could converse comfortably without invading any personal space. A part of Errante wished he could be closer, but he did not reveal that desire.

"How may I help?" he asked instead.

After a moment, Rafe drew in a deep breath. "Something happened, and… I don't know what to think. Or how I feel about it."

Errante raised a brow. "I think it is obvious you feel disturbed. Please, continue. I would like to help."

For several long moments, Rafe looked at him, and Errante had a hard time reading the complicated mix of emotions that played across Rafe's expressive face. "It was on our off day. I went into the town with Simeon. It was fine, nothing special — I bought a book, had a drink and something to eat in one of the pubs. Then… well, there was a man watching me." Rafe's cheeks grew flushed, and he lowered his gaze. "I'm not…. It was obvious what he wanted. But I wasn't interested." He glanced up quickly. "Not that I'm not interested in sex, I mean. Of course I am. He was good looking, just… not my type." His face grew even redder at the admission.

Errante nodded. "I am aware of your preferences, Rafael. You need not feel uncomfortable with me." For some reason, Rafe seemed agitated about the admission, and Errante decided a small return of trust wouldn't hurt — how could it? It wasn't as though he had acted upon it in millennia, or intended to do so, and it might make Rafe feel more at ease. "If it makes you feel better, I have always preferred male partners as well."

"You do?" Rafe's dark eyes widened, but then he looked away again. "Well. I left the pub, heading back home. But apparently the man had followed me. He was insulting, I'm sure nothing you haven't heard before, about people in carnivals being too good for the locals. He was angry I turned him down."

"That is on him, not you," Errante said at once. He felt an irrational desire to return to that world and track the man down, perhaps give him some 'help' along his Path that he wouldn't appreciate. It was, of course, a mad idea. But the thought of anyone hurting Rafe, be it physically or emotionally, roused a protective fury within him.

"I know." Indeed, Rafe seemed certain on that front. Then he ran a hand through his hair, a sign of agitation Errante had never seen him use before. "It wasn't that. He attacked me, drew a knife, which didn't worry me. I know how to defend myself. I knocked the knife away. But… things happened."

There was tension in Rafe's shoulders, and Errante longed to put a comforting arm around them. But for the moment, all he had for reassurance were his words. "What happened?"

Rafe stood up and began to pace, his agitation growing. "I had him in a hold, intending to render him unconscious and slip away. But he had another knife, one I hadn't seen. And he stabbed me in the abdomen. Then... I'm not sure how to describe it."

Alarmed, Errante watched Rafe stride back and forth across the rug. He wanted to jump up and demand Rafe show him the wound, allow him to heal it, but he stopped himself. Rafe didn't act like he was in pain. Had he sought a potion from Peter?

"Just go slowly. I am here and listening."

Drawing in a ragged breath, Rafe nodded. "I thought I was dying. I felt hot, like I was burning all over. I dropped the man and went to my knees. I wanted to stop the bleeding, but when I moved my hands to my body... it's like it wasn't there. My vision was all white, and I don't know how long I knelt there, but then... I was back, somehow. My clothes were gone, and so was the wound. The guy regained consciousness, and his neck looked red, his clothes were singed, but I didn't stick around. I picked up the coat I'd lost in the fight, grabbed my book, and came back home. But it's been bothering me ever since." He paused and looked at Errante. "It wasn't you, was it? You've said you can't help us outside the Carnival, but did you do something to me?"

Errante stood, then moved to Rafe. He needed to comfort him, needed to reassure him. "No, I swear," he said, putting his hands on Rafe's shoulders. They were much the same height, but Rafe's shoulders were broad, even with the exaggerated effect of the Ringmaster's coat. "Are you worried I was interfering in your life away from the Carnival?"

"No!" Rafe was panting. "I hoped it *had* been you, to be honest. But deep down, I know it wasn't. It was me. Something in me. But I don't know what!"

Seeing Rafe in turmoil, when he was normally so strong, so resilient, was more than Errante could bear. He put his hands on Rafe's shoulders, gripping them firmly. "Stop. This is not something for you to fear. It simply means you must have magic you were never aware of before. We have known since you were a child that you had abilities, have we not?"

"Yes…" Rafe drew in a deep breath, and he looked into Errante's eyes as though searching for answers. "But this was… unsettling. I *hurt* someone. I don't know if I could have killed him without meaning to."

"It was not your fault." Errante shook Rafe gently. He'd seen magical trauma before — some people were dismayed or even frightened to learn something about themselves that they hadn't known. Persephone had dealt with it more than he had himself, but she'd told him it could disturb a person's sense of self as much to gain something unexpectedly as to suffer a loss in the same way, especially if the realization was through violence. "Listen to me. Magic manifests in different ways for different people. Some are born to their abilities, as I was, as Persephone and Mephistopheles were. Others come into them slowly, often as adolescents or young adults — that will be the case with the young girl to whom you gave the token, if you will remember. Still others only manifest in extremis — when their life or the life of someone they love is endangered — or at least if they perceive it to be endangered. I know you have been a witness to that, here in the carnival, for it has happened before and it will again."

Rafe seemed to calm down; his breathing slowed, and the creases on his forehead eased as he listened to Errante's words. "Do you really think that could be it?"

"I do." Errante offered a reassuring smile. What he really

wanted to do was to pull Rafe into his arms, to offer the reassurance he seemed to need so desperately.

Then the frown lines came back, and Rafe looked confused once more. "Why didn't Persephone warn me? Or… or you? You both know so much. You must have seen this in my future since I was a child."

"Actually, we could not." When Rafe protested, Errante shook his head. He wanted Rafe to understand, or at least as much as Errante himself understood. "Please, hear me out. I was not saying we knew and did not tell you. I am telling you that neither of us knew either. Your Path and your Fate are hidden from us. They have been since we brought you into the Carnival as little more than an infant. Since you never asked, we never felt it necessary to tell you. I have not known why, and I still am uncertain, but given this manifestation of yours, and whatever your abilities and powers are becoming now, I believe that to be a part of it. A shield, if you will. Perhaps in the same way that your mind blocked the memories of your first home, it also blocked your powers and protected you from discovery. No doubt the recent assault, and specifically the wound you took, triggered a survival instinct which broke through that block and manifested in the way you needed to save your life."

"Oh." Rafe stood there, obviously nonplussed, but Errante could see he was processing the information. Of course, Errante had no way to prove he was correct, but he'd seen more things than the vast majority of beings in the multiverse, and he was well aware of situations similar to this. Many of them, unfortunately, had ended in tragedy, but he would not allow that to happen to Rafe. No matter what it cost him.

"And to get back to what happened to you that started this, I will point out that you did not kill your attacker — apparently your instinct was not to destroy, no matter what had been done to you. That speaks of a nobility of spirit, Rafael. Be proud of that. And as for your newly awakened powers… well, we can work with you on that. If you are worried about unexpected things happening, ones that you feel you cannot control, remember that my magic will check yours, and keep anyone from coming to harm."

"It will?" The hope and relief on Rafe's face was heartbreaking. The man had obviously been driving himself to distraction with the fear that whatever he'd done was going to turn him into some deranged killer. But Errante felt safe in his reassurances; the magic of the Carnival was strong and true to his will.

"Yes." Errante replied simply and with complete certainty.

Rafe closed his eyes, drawing in a deep breath. He remained that way for several moments before opening his eyes again to look at Errante with gratitude. "Thank you. Thank you for the reassurance, and for… well, for seeking me out and asking me to talk. I didn't know how to approach it, and instead of going away the way I wanted it to, it just kept eating at me. I wasn't sure what to do until you approached me."

"I know what it is to be torn apart by worries and dark thoughts." Errante felt his jaw clench unconsciously, and he forced himself to smile instead. "But I am glad I could help to ease your mind. Although now you need to determine where you wish to go from here. Once awakened, your power is unlikely to disappear again. You need some training, and some practice in containing your power and forming it to your will. As good as your instinctive control seems to be, you need to know what you are working with."

"I guess you're right." Rafe became pensive again. "Can you… will you be the one to train me? This doesn't seem like Persephone's type of magic, and I am quite aware most of what Mephistopheles is doing is pure illusion. Peter's magic is all in his potions, so…"

Errante hesitated — did Rafe perhaps not wish him as a teacher? "I would be honored, although I am not actually your only choice. I know many wizards on many worlds, and I am sure we could find one who would suit you, if that is what you wish. It would mean leaving the Carnival for a time, of course, but you could always return." He didn't want Rafe to go, but he would not force him to stay if he wished to go elsewhere. Even if it would tear Errante's heart from his chest if it happened.

"No! I mean, no, thank you," Rafe said quickly. "I want to be here, and I'd like it if you were the one to train me."

It was Errante's turn to be relieved, though he tried not to show it. Instead, he nodded. "If that is your wish, then that is what we shall do. If you like, we will start this evening, after our patrons have departed."

"All right." Rafe hesitated, and then placed his hands on Errante's arms, where Errante still gripped his shoulders. "Again, thank you. You've already helped me so much, and now you're helping again. I literally owe you my life."

For a time Errante simply looked at Rafe, indulging himself in being closer to Rafe than he'd ever been. Few people ever touched him, and this being the man who meant more to him than anyone else made him want to savor the contact for as long as he could.

Finally, however, Errante stepped back before he could become lost in the warmth of Rafe's presence. "You are, of course, welcome."

Rafe nodded, then hesitated, as though he might actually be reluctant to leave. "I suppose I should get back to work. I'll see you tonight, then?"

Errante inclined his head. "I shall be near the front, as I usually am."

"Right. I'll see you later."

With a final smile, Rafe turned and walked toward the door. After a moment, Errante heard it open, then quietly close once more. Leaving him alone with his thoughts.

As glad as he was that Rafe wished to remain, there was much to think about. The power he sensed in Rafe when they had touched was stronger than any he'd felt in a very long time. Given the treachery of his great enemy, however, there was always a chance that this was an elaborate trap, and that by aiding Rafe in this, Errante was sealing his own doom. Yet there were Persephone's words from long ago to consider. If this was Rafe's hidden Path, Errante must help him navigate it, no matter what dangers lay ahead.

And there would always be danger, no matter what Errante did. Even if he couldn't see his own Path, he knew that inevitably it would lead to only one place — and when it did, there would be death.

CHAPTER 5

As he watched the last of the happy people leaving the Carnival, hands full of trinkets or bags of treats, Rafe finally allowed himself a moment to breathe. Ever since he'd left Errante's trailer earlier that day, he'd been overwhelmed with tasks that needed his attention. He wondered, now, if Errante might have had a little something to do with that. Even though Rafe felt very much relieved after their talk, he might have been tempted to dwell on things if he'd been less occupied with his work.

As the last people left — they never had to announce that the Carnival was closing, it was part of Errante's magic that made people decide to leave of their own accord — the roustabouts began picking up bits of debris from the grounds and the food vendors cleaned up their own areas. The lights of the Carousel and the big Ferris wheel winked out, and the music, which played constantly in the background trailed off into silence. He spotted Errante approaching him, and Rafe's heart beat faster at the sight.

"I have made a place for us to explore your magic where

you do not need to feel constrained because you are in fear of causing damage or hurting anyone."

"That sounds perfect." Rafe smiled. After the fear he'd experienced because of this apparent awakening of his magic, he found he was looking forward to what might be a great deal of one-on-one time with Errante. He'd have gone through the experience again willingly had he known this would be the result.

Errante beckoned for him to follow, then headed toward the red and white striped canvas of the Big Top. The Galliers' last show had been over for hours, so it would be deserted.

When they stepped through the flaps of the entrance, however, Rafe was a bit surprised to see that the trapeze was gone, as were the seats where the crowds had been cheering only an hour before. The space was now open and empty, even the sawdust of the floor having been replaced by bare earth. Errante moved to the center, under the highest peak of the tent — which now had no pole to hold it up, yet it remained a peak — and turned to face Rafe.

"No one else can enter," Errante said. He gestured around the tent. "There is nothing here that can be destroyed, no matter what we discover about your magic."

"Do you really think it's strong enough to be worried?" Rafe asked. He frowned, feeling a bit of trepidation.

Errante spread his hands. "It is best to be safe, is it not? Perhaps your magic is only defensive and protective, in which case this is unnecessary. Yet I think it is likely more than that. It was strong enough to hide your Path from me and obscure your Fate from Persephone. We are both quite old and our magics are honed to a purpose. I have met a few mages who have been able to block my power, but not many. And I have met none in a long time."

Not for the first time, Rafe wondered how old Errante

actually was, though he wasn't quite impertinent enough to ask. No doubt Errante would reply with something suitably accurate yet completely incomprehensible, anyway. That was how he answered most questions about his past to anyone who dared ask.

"All right, I trust you — you know what you're doing, and I do not."

"Then let us begin." Errante said simply. "You can do various tricks. This I have seen. They are small magics, but they may give us a hint where your talents lie. Show me."

Rafe nodded, then held up a hand, concentrating for a moment before producing a small flame in the palm of his hand. He passed it back and forth, then produced another, and another, until he had five small flames flickering. Then he tossed them up in the air and juggled them as though they were the balls the clowns used. After a few moments, he dropped his hands, and the flames died out. "That's the best one I have," he admitted. "I tried to go up from there, but producing a sixth flame makes me tired. The only other use I've found for this is that I can always keep my coffee warm — provided it isn't in a paper cup!"

That made Errante chuckle. "So your magic is linked to fire — or more accurately, to energy, as Nik would no doubt say. He manipulates energy as well. In fact, he is the one who keeps all the mechanicals going, rather than myself. I could do it, and in fact, I did it myself before his Path led him here, but it is what makes him happy, so it became his job. He is very proud of what he does here."

"I never realized," Rafe replied. He was surprised, but then again, Nik the engineer was even quieter and more private than Errante. There was a sadness about him that little seemed to lighten. Apparently, there were even more silent secrets in the Carnival than he had yet learned, even after having lived in it and known its inhabitants for almost his entire life.

"Everyone has their secrets," Errante said softly. "But this explains what occurred when you were attacked. You simply manipulated energy in a new way, which explains why your attacker was burned and your clothes disappeared. Energy is a transfer. Some mages, like Nik, hold it within themselves, and can build up a sort of storehouse in their bodies, like a battery. It is no doubt why you can manage five flames, but not six — it uses up the store and leaves you weak. Nik has a larger store, but even he does not power the lights and Carousel just from within. He transfers the psychic energy from the crowd, in part, and the waste heat from the concessions. He even uses the heat produced by every person, which would radiate out into the world unnoticed. It is his very special talent."

"I see, or at least I have a grasp of what you're saying." Rafe chuckled. "Calliope wasn't as enthusiastic about the sciences as the arts, but I've read quite a bit, since it interested me." He paused. "So, I suppose I used up my 'battery' and consumed my clothing to fuel whatever happened?" It probably also explained why he had been so exhausted afterward. He'd slept the rest of that day and night, only waking the following morning.

"Exactly." Errante smiled, obviously pleased. "You should be able to increase your 'battery' with practice, and we will explore how you converted your garments into energy. That was more active than what Nik does. His talent is to transfer energy that is already being produced elsewhere. You did something that is more difficult. You directly converted matter to energy. While Nik could use the energy if someone burned something near him, he cannot go directly from matter to energy."

"So how do I increase my 'battery'?" Rafe asked.

"First, you need to find that place within yourself where the energy resides." Errante smiled. "Which is going to require you to follow your instincts. Produce a flame once more."

Rafe held up a hand and did it. It was smaller than the ones he had produced before, but he did it. "Now what?"

"You are drawing energy from within. Move your focus from the flame itself and follow its path inside. If it helps, visualize it coming from within your body, just like a battery. Perhaps your heart, or your liver, or even your brain."

Rafe closed his eyes and tried to expand his awareness. He could see the flame in his mind, picturing it in his hand. After thinking for a moment, since he'd never really given much consideration to how the flames were produced, he thought about the point in his hand being something like a wick, pulling the energy to make the flame from inside his body. But instead of feeling a pull to a specific organ such as Errante described, it felt more like it was coming from his entire body.

"I don't think it's working," he said, opening his eyes and seeing the flame flicker and die. "Maybe I drained it too much already?"

Frowning, Errante stepped closer. He seemed to hesitate for a moment. "May I take your hands?" he asked. "I can help with that."

"Of course." Rafe drew in a breath, telling himself not to let himself get carried away from the thought of Errante touching him. It had been so tempting earlier that day to step closer when Errante had put his hands on Rafe's shoulders, but this was even more intimate. But he held out his hands, pleased that they weren't trembling.

Errante took Rafe's hands in his own warm ones, palms touching. He could feel Errante's long, elegant fingers closing over his, and then Errante stepped closer and closed his own eyes.

For a moment, Rafe gazed at Errante's face. They'd rarely stood so close to one another, and he had never noticed that Errante's lashes were so thick and dark. Up close, his olive skin was still as smooth as a young man's — or as Rafe's own. Then Rafe's attention was drawn down to their joined hands, where he could feel something akin to an electric current flowing out of Errante and into him. He drew in a sharp breath at the sensation of energy coursing through him. The fatigue he had felt but had ignored disappeared, and he suddenly felt as he did when he'd had several cups of coffee with sugar. He was almost buzzing with energy, felt as though he could fly like the Galliers, or lift more weight than Samson.

The sensation was amazing, and when Errante's eyes opened, Rafe stared into them, seeing entire galaxies whirling in those dark depths, and bursts of energy that he thought were stars being consumed in destruction. But he saw life in them, too, other stars being born in flares of their own. He wanted to fall into Errante's eyes and see the secrets of the universe revealed before him, to know the magic Errante saw when he looked out at the world.

Then Errante blinked, and Rafe came back to himself. He dropped Errante's hands, severing the connection. It couldn't have lasted more than a heartbeat, but Rafe could still feel the energy coursing through him.

"What was that?" he asked, breathing hard.

"I transferred some of my magic to you," Errante replied. He tilted his head to one side, regarding Rafe with what seemed to be surprise. "You could take a bit more than I was expecting. Are you all right?"

"I... I think so." Rafe felt like he could go out and run a marathon. "Just... hyped up, I suppose."

Errante's brow furrowed, his expression sliding into concern. "Take deep breaths. You will be fine in a few moments," he said. "It feels intense the first time it happens. I should have warned you."

Intense *was one word for it*, Rafe thought. But as he continued to take deliberately measured breaths, the buzzing slowly settled down. He still felt energetic, but it was more the way he felt after a restful sleep. But now that he was 'recharged', so to speak, he could sense what Errante had meant by a focus on the upper right side of his abdomen. He could feel the energy pooling there, but far stronger than anything he'd ever felt.

"I think I feel that 'battery' you mentioned," he said, touching the area gingerly.

"Ah." Errante nodded, seeming unsurprised. "The liver. My… my people believed it was the repository of the soul. By chance, is that where your assailant stabbed you?"

Rafe's eyes grew wide. "How did you know?"

Errante spread his hands. "It would explain how your magic so easily healed you, without you even realizing it. Instinctive self protection, without you even having to focus on it. If he had cut your hand or your leg, you might not have healed yourself. I do recall you getting bumps and scrapes enough as a child, from what Calliope moaned about when she took you outside the Carnival."

"I did indeed, and no, I can't recall ever healing myself before," Rafe said slowly.

Errante was watching him closely. "Do you feel like continuing? If that was too much for you, we can stop here, let you recover, and think through things."

Rafe wanted to keep going, but more than that, he wanted Errante to touch him again, with or without the magical recharge involved. But since he couldn't say that, he simply nodded. "We can keep going."

The energy he had absorbed proved to be greater than he'd imagined. He could produce not simply a small flame, but an actual palm full of fire at Errante's direction.

"Now toss it up in the air, and see if you can keep it suspended."

Rafe did as Errante asked, but once it reached the top of the arc, it fell back down, despite Rafe's concentration on having it float. Errante ran him through the exercise a few more times, and he could finally stop it in mid-air without touching it. The ball of fire hovered briefly between them, then fizzled out with a soft pop.

"That is enough for one evening," Errante said into the stillness. "You have done very well. We learned what your magic is and where it resides. Now it is a matter of practice and slow building of your 'battery'."

"What happens then?" Rafe asked.

"That is up to you," Errante replied quietly. "There are many paths to magic, and it can take a mage years, if not decades, to explore his abilities and hone them to where he can instinctively do whatever he desires within his realm. As you gain confidence, we can determine what you can do to channel energy as Nik does."

Rafe nodded. "I guess it only makes sense to go slowly and carefully."

"It does," Errante agreed. "Even though I was born to my magic, it took me many years of practice and study before I ever dared attempt to step across the multiverse."

There were so many questions Rafe wanted to ask. Errante had given him these tiny glimpses into his past, and it made him want to know more. What had Errante been like as a young man? Had he ever been in love? Had he ever doubted himself or worried that his magic might harm someone else?

But he simply nodded again. "I guess I'll charge up overnight?"

Errante smiled. "That is how it works. In whatever way you naturally recharge your magic, it has been happening for years, and will continue to happen. Perhaps even faster, now that you are aware of it. In fact, that is a task I shall set for you. Take note of anything you feel might aid you in charging. Do not *try* to pull energy to you yet. It can have unexpected consequences. But if there is anything that makes you feel more energetic, or that you notice makes you able to manifest your flames better or faster, take note."

"All right." Rafe wondered how he could tell, but since he'd never even known he was doing it before, perhaps it would become obvious now that he was paying attention. "I suppose that means we are finished."

"I think that you have absorbed enough for one session." Errante looked amused. "I know you would most likely prefer to continue, but slowly, Rafael. We do not wish to burn you out just as you are getting started."

"I suppose not." Rafe was less interested in continuing the magic lesson, however, than in continuing to spend time with Errante, so he seized upon the most obvious thing. "Are you going to restore the Big Top?"

"I am, or else the Galliers might be perturbed to find their equipment missing," Errante replied, his tone full of amusement.

"Can I watch? You know, to see how you do your own magic."

One of the odd things about Errante was that although they all lived amid his magic, which sustained them, moved them from place to place, and formed the very essence of the Carnival around them, Errante rarely demonstrated his magic openly. No one had ever, as far as Rafe knew, witnessed the

Carnival being moved, nor how it was transformed to suit its location. Errante's work always seemed to be from the shadows, almost never openly. It was as though his magic was as obscure as his past, and even though he had charged up Rafe's 'battery', it had been something far more felt than seen.

Errante hesitated, but then inclined his head. "Very well, if you think it would be of interest."

"Actually, it would." Rafe couldn't contain his smile, and he hoped he didn't look as eager as he felt.

Errante lifted his hands without replying, and Rafe watched as the central support of the Big Top appeared as though it had never been gone. The rest of the equipment shimmered into view, the trapeze, the bleachers, even the sawdust on the floor. In the space of three deep breaths, the Big Top was restored.

"Your magic is obviously different from mine," Rafe said slowly. "You aren't changing things. Are you simply making them appear?"

"I made them move." Errante said. "Objects can have a Path just as living beings do. So I sent them to another place, then brought them back. Do not strain your head too much about the how at this moment — but I work under the same magical laws that you must. So does Persephone, and her magic differs from both of ours. You will learn, Rafael. Give yourself time."

Rafe wanted to know more, but he doubted that pushing Errante would get him anywhere. And he was also feeling tired, which shouldn't surprise him. He'd done more magic in the last two hours than he had in his life, as well as dealt with his regular duties, so it wasn't just his magical battery that felt drained.

As they stepped out of the Big Top, Errante pointed toward the area where Rafe's quarters were. "Sleep now. I will bid you a good night," he said quietly, then turned away toward the other end of the Carnival.

"Good night," Rafe replied softly. He watched Errante walk away, then seem to almost disappear in the shadows of the now-dark Midway. Someday, perhaps, Rafe would make that walk with him. Then neither of them would ever have to be alone.

"Are you mad?"

Errante raised a brow at Rafe's protest. He couldn't help but be amused at Rafe's look of outrage, even if it was misplaced.

"Not the last time I checked. Well, I have never been professionally analyzed, if I am being truthful," he replied, keeping his expression grave.

"An assassin? Really? You have allowed a killer, an actual bloodletting, murdering *assassin* into the Carnival?"

"Errante knows what he's doing, Rafe," Persephone chimed in. Unlike Errante, she didn't even try to hide her smile.

The three of them were standing to one side of the Midway as the gates opened for the day, admitting a flood of people, as usual. Rafe would normally have been starting his typical walk down the Midway, advertising the shows and attractions. But circumstances had made it so that Errante had to brief him on something that was to occur later, so that it wouldn't catch him unaware.

Rafe looked skeptical, running a hand through his hair. "I

don't see how..." he said, then trailed off with a frown. "It's not really about the assassin, is it?"

"Of course not." Errante allowed the smile he'd been withholding to curve his lips. "Someone else's Path requires the assassin. This is no surprise to me, or to Persephone, who warned me about it when we arrived on this world. I am warning you, so you will not be alarmed at anything that happens. Rest assured, no one is in any actual danger from this. I know exactly where she is and what she is up to — and I do not think she will be happy about where her Path eventually leads." He paused and grew more serious. "I am not pleased either, if I am being honest. In addition to the assassin, I had to permit an evil mage to perform magic in *my* Carnival. I have rarely encountered a Path quite so... *unusual* as the one we are here to aid, but I only aid the Traveler. I do not determine the Path."

He glanced at Persephone, who held up her hands. "Don't look at me. Like you, I only read the Fate. I don't set it. If you want to lodge a complaint, you'll have to find this world's equivalent of my sister, if one exists."

Errante chuckled. "We shall leave that for an actual emergency," he replied. Then he glanced back at Rafe, who was frowning between the two of them and obviously perturbed. "Softly, Rafael. There are twists and turns to magic that we have all had to learn to navigate, and you will have to learn them as well. This is unusual, yes, but not unheard of. We shall do what we must, then be on our way. And we shall keep going with your lessons."

Every evening for the last few days, he had taken Rafael to the Big Top after the Carnival closed, and trained with him, teaching Rafael to work with his magic and push it further. He could now conjure and make a ring of fire around the interior of the Big Top, and manifest as many small balls of fire as he desired to juggle. He could keep the flames going for longer and feel less drained at the end of each lesson. But Errante was guiding him slowly indeed. There was great power in Rafe, and while Rafe couldn't do anything to harm Errante directly, it was best for Rafe to go at the pace with which he was most comfortable.

Rafe nodded, seeming relieved. "All right. I will trust that older heads — I will not speculate on them being any wiser — know what's best." He perched his top hat on his head. "I guess I'd better get to work." With that, he set off into the crowd, his booming voice encouraging people to head to the Big Top for the first performance of the day.

"Do not forget the Grand Parade will be at one this afternoon, instead of five," Errante called after him. Rafe tossed a long-suffering look back at him over his shoulder, before continuing on his way. Disruptions to the schedule were not something Rafe appreciated.

"Walk with me," Persephone said, raising a hand to indicate the end of the Midway where her tent was located. Errante nodded, offered her his arm, then set out toward the purple tent, set, as always, a way beyond the others to offer a bit more privacy.

"Was there something on your mind, or did you simply desire the pleasure of my company?" Errante asked, his tone gently teasing.

"Actually, there is something," she said. She glanced around at the carnival goers, all of whom were eagerly exploring the games, rides, and concessions. "I think you may wish to consider what to do when Rafe approaches you about returning to the world of his birth."

Surprised, Errante stopped, looking down at her. "Do you think it is likely?" he asked. He wasn't certain how he felt about returning there, as horrible as the first stop had been. "In all these years, he has never asked. Have you Seen him doing so now?"

"No, I haven't." She pulled at his arm, and he started forward again. "I'm simply a student of human nature, my friend. Just because he hasn't been interested in his past before doesn't mean he'll want it to remain a mystery forever. I assume you could find it again, even if you can't read Rafe's Path?"

"I could," he replied slowly.

"Look, I understand why you might not want to do it." This time she was the one to stop, and she looked up at him. "You're afraid that Rafe is the one who burned that village, aren't you?"

Errante drew in a breath. "Yes." He whispered the word, but Persephone had, with a rapier thrust of insight, pinned his own fear. "He is a mage who manipulates fire. I sense much deeper power in him than he has shown, but I suppose I was avoiding thinking too deeply about linking the burned village to his newly manifested powers."

She tapped his arm, and her tone was dry. "You love him, Errante, whether or not you want to admit it to me. And if you and I — and, I suspect, everyone who saw that village — can make the link, Rafe will certainly be able to as well. Calliope only told him that his village was destroyed, and he was the lone survivor. But having seen those bodies with my own eyes, I can tell you the people were dead before they were burned."

"You are certain of that?" Errante looked into her eyes, seeking the truth. "He was not the one who killed them? Because I will not return him to that place, even if he requests it, if there is any chance he will feel guilty for what happened there." He could not say more, or explain why, since to tell her of the attack Rafe experienced would be to violate Rafe's trust.

"He may have burned the village — in fear, I suspect — but fire doesn't sever limbs and heads, nor leave bodies gutted in the middle of their homes. The only people who were burned to death in the fire were the actual murderers of that village. No doubt when they killed Rafe's family, the child reacted with understandable terror."

Given what had happened to Rafe less than a week before, it was possible the attackers had even tried to kill Rafe, and he'd saved himself and destroyed them. But it eased Errante's mind to know that Rafe would never have to feel guilty if he ever wanted to return to the world of his birth.

He started walking again. "Thank you. I never asked, because it did not seem relevant, but you are right. He will make the link, so I must make sure, before I agree to return him to that place, that he knows he is in no way responsible for what happened."

"Good."

They continued on in silence until they reached her tent. He turned, took one of her hands, and bent over it to kiss it. "Thank you, my friend. I have no idea how I could have survived all these long years without your counsel."

Smiling, she tapped him on the hand. "You would have done fine, but if I've made your own Path a little less wearisome, I'll consider that some small payback for what I owe *you*."

"Never count debts between friends," he replied. Then he gave her a courteous bow. "Now I will leave you to dispense your wisdom to others who need it. It would be selfish to keep your counsel all for myself."

"Save your for charm the mortals," she replied tartly, but she was smiling. "Or better yet, for Rafe."

He shook his head, then turned away and headed back toward the ticket booth. He had much to do to make sure his Travelers did as they needed to do.

The small drama of the attempted assassination played out in the Big Top while Errante watched, finding himself envious of the young Guardian being and his water spirit mate. The two were so obviously in love, and their Paths intertwined with simple strength.

When it was finally over, he moved to where Rafe stood near the performer's entrance. The dagger the failed assassin had used still lay in the sawdust, so Errante picked it up. A dagger bespelled to never miss — even though it obviously *had* — might be of use to someone else.

"We have a task to do — one that I think will ease your mind on this episode," he said softly. "Come."

Rafe looked curious, but he didn't question the summons. Errante led him to Gentleman Jim's tent, where the blonde-haired, blue-eyed assassin, who had been masquerading as the knife-thrower's assistant, had retreated after her failure. She had changed back to her regular clothes, and was just slipping on a set of low-heeled pumps when Errante and Rafe entered.

She looked surprised, but before she could speak, Errante waved a hand, and she froze in place.

"What do you want to do with her?" Rafe asked, looking at the woman with disapproval. "She's a killer. Are you going to turn her over to the authorities here?"

"No, this world's humans do not believe in magic, and I do not believe the penalties she faces for her failure are quite suitable in this case. Her Path goes… elsewhere."

The woman could not move, but she was still aware, and it wasn't difficult for Errante to read the fear in her eyes. He took one of her arms, gesturing for Rafe to take the other, and then they walked her out of the tent as though she were a very lifelike doll. Given it was a Carnival, people looked at them curiously, but obviously thought it was just another act. Some even pointed and applauded.

"The Funhouse?" Rafe asked as Errante guided them toward the building, the grinning clown-mouth opening yawning before them. "Are you going to set her up as a display?"

"Now, what kind of lesson would that be?" Errante asked with a snort of amusement. "If it were up to me, I would put her in the haunted house and let the ghosts of the murdered spirits show her the error of her ways. But, alas, she is destined for someplace she will like even less. She might even come to wish I was the type of person who took lives as well."

They entered the funhouse, which had stopped its typical mad gyrations when Errante stepped through the entrance. Without the usual distractions of the place, it took only a few moments to walk through to the "Emergency Exit" at the rear.

"Put her down here for a moment," he said, and he and Rafe lowered her so her feet were on the ground. She wasn't very tall, and even though the magical paralysis held her still, her forehead was damp with sweat.

Errante stood in front of her, looking into her eyes. "Murder, especially paid-for, sanctioned murder, is evil," he said sternly. "We of the Carnival do not kill, even when it could be justified by some. Instead, we shall simply do as we do for all Travelers and help you along your Path — and please remember, you came to this point via your own actions. You could have turned aside at any point. We all shape our destinies with our free will. Now you shall discover your fate."

With that, he stepped back, pulling open the exit door. The land outside was so bright it was almost surreal. The cloudless sky could not have been bluer, the grass could not have been greener, stretching out lushly as far as the eye could see. Of people, there was no sign, but there was a single road that wound through the field, its pale amber surface gleaming, right from the base of the exit.

"If you would, please, Rafael," he said, holding the door open.

"My pleasure," Rafe replied, a wealth of satisfaction in his tone. He picked the assassin up, stepped to the edge of the doorway, then lowered her onto the road.

"Choose your future Path wisely," Errante said, waving a hand to release her from the paralysis. She whirled to stare at them, and Errante simply smiled. "And pray to whatever gods you may believe in that no one drops a house on you."

With that, he let the door close and turned to Rafe.

"Feel better now?" he asked and was rewarded by Rafe's grin.

"I'll never doubt you again."

CHAPTER 7

Rafe felt the magic coursing through him, and he focused, as Errante had taught him, on shaping the energy to his will. Holding up his hands, he "pulled" from the storehouse within himself, letting it flow up and out through his fingertips. Obedient to his control, the flames shaped into a sphere.

"Rather than quantity, we shall try for quality this time. Try making the sphere hotter and smaller."

Errante was standing a few feet away, observing Rafe with focused concentration. He stood as still as a statue, dark eyes narrowed slightly, hands clasped behind his back. Under the lights of the big top, his black hair had a blue cast, and the warm tone of his skin looked even darker. Rafe was used to being watched — he was Ringmaster and so being the center of attention was nothing new. Yet it was far more intimate to be the subject of Errante's intense regard, and the warmth that stole over him as he gazed back had little to do with the flames in his hands.

It felt as though as his magical abilities slowly grew under Errante's tutelage, so did the pull he felt toward Errante. He'd lived with his feelings for Errante for years, of course, but something, somehow, had changed since his magic had manifested. What had been a sort of yearning from afar had deepened, and now he felt a pull that was becoming harder to resist with each day that passed. The more time he spent with Errante, the more he felt compelled to spend. Perhaps that was the tipping point — what had begun as a yearning was developing into an increasingly powerful need. Now it had grown to where all he could think of in the morning when he woke was getting ready so he could hurry to get his first sight of Errante. Even his dreams were haunted by images of them together, naked bodies entwined, and now not a day seemed to pass when Rafe didn't wake up so hard with desire, it was a physical pain.

"Your concentration is not the best this evening. Is there something disturbing you?"

The erotic images which had filled his dreams were hard to dispel, so it took a moment for Rafe to register what Errante had said. He blinked in surprise as he realized that the ball of flame, instead of condensing and becoming yellow as it should, had expanded and turned redder and cooler. Which, of course, it would, if he wasn't concentrating. An increase in entropy when focus was lost, Errante had explained early in their lessons, was as true for magic as for any other system in the multiverse. It was why a mage must train their will intently to maintain an effect, especially at first. Otherwise, there could be unintended consequences.

"I'm sorry," Rafe replied guiltily, relieved that mind reading apparently wasn't among the several magics Errante seemed to do as easily as breathing. He allowed the ball to continue to expand and cool until it dissipated completely. It was easier to conjure another than to pull one back that had expanded that far. "I promise I'll try to do better."

"You can burn out as easily from overdoing magic as from

exercising your body to exhaustion," Errante replied, seeming unperturbed. "We have been practicing every day for several weeks now, and you also work hard all day, every day, performing your duties for the Carnival. You are likely in need of a break, and for that I apologize, as I should have considered it sooner. Perhaps we should stop here, and you can rest for a few nights before we begin again."

"I don't want a break," Rafe said quickly. "I enjoy the lessons. Really, it's nothing for you to apologize for, Errante. This is important to me."

"Hm." Errante stroked his chin with one long finger, seeming to consider. "I have no wish to deny you, if you desire to continue. You have been working diligently on manifesting your power, but perhaps it would not be as draining if we were to change focus. We should switch gears for a bit and find how to increase your reserves."

That caught Rafe's interest. He could tell the amount of magic he could store within himself was growing, as evidenced by the way he could produce more flames and hold them longer. Errante had told him to imagine his store not as a battery, which had a limit that could not be exceeded, but more like a body of water. It might seem small at first, like a puddle on the ground, but it could grow and grow, becoming a pond, then a lake, perhaps even an ocean.

At the moment, Rafe sort of felt he was working more on the puddle size. Which wasn't bad, considering that when he'd started, it had probably been more like a few drops. Errante had repeatedly urged him to go slowly, and even with his limited knowledge of magic, he knew enough to be cautious.

"What do you suggest?" he asked. Taking a chance, he crossed the Big Top to where Errante stood, wanting to be closer.

"We can start with learning what will 'recharge' you,

other than sleep." Errante frowned in thought, then motioned for Rafe to follow him outside the Big Top. "It is quiet now, and almost everyone has settled in for the night. Walk with me."

I'd follow you anywhere. The thought came unbidden, and Rafe wished he could voice it. How would Errante react?

Since he couldn't speak the words he wished to, Rafe simply nodded. "Of course."

Soon they were walking down the dark and quiet Midway. "Let us try what works for Nik. Close your eyes. Try to sense the energy of the Carnival. The ebb is low right now, granted, but we hardly want to have you inundated."

Rafe did as he was bidden. He tried to imagine the surrounding energies. There was a hum that came from generators Errante had said were of Nik's own design, which consumed only the magic Nik put into them, but Rafe couldn't feel anything 'magical' coming from them he could tap into. He knew there was a magical boundary around the Carnival, but while he could sense it with some instinct he'd not fully developed yet, it was simply *there*, not something that he felt he could pull from. There were glimmers of magic all around the Carnival grounds, the rides, the prizes in the game booths, and many of the people he could sense distantly. And, of course, there was Errante, who seemed to almost glow with magic.

"I can feel the magic, but I don't seem to have an actual connection to it, if that makes sense," Rafe said slowly, opening his eyes and looking at Errante in consternation. "Is that bad?"

Errante chuckled, shaking his head. "No, it simply means we have not found your 'source' yet." He looked up into the sky, where a waxing gibbous moon shone brightly, casting a silver light over everything. "Try focusing on the moon and its light. What do you feel from it?"

Rafe closed his eyes once more and directed his attention upward. This time, it was different. There was energy in that pale light. It was a bare trickle, but he could feel it like a cool caress over his skin, absorbing into his inner "puddle." It was something he'd never experienced before, and it awoke in him a sense of wonder. How often over his life had he stood in the moonlight, but never known it was recharging him?

"The moon? That's my source?" He asked, looking at Errante once more. "It's not very strong, though. If it recharges me, it would probably take a long time, if that makes sense."

"It does, but I do not believe the moon is what we seek," Errante was staring back at him, then he stepped closer. Rafe had doffed his Ringmaster coat before meeting for the lesson, and he stood now in only a plain white shirt, the sleeves rolled up to just below his elbows. Errante placed a warm hand on Rafe's arm, then closed his own eyes. "No. Not the moon, rather the sun. A moon is merely a reflection of the sun, which is why it feels so weak to you."

"The sun?" Rafe looked at him in surprise. "Shouldn't I have felt that before, then? It's not like I've been avoiding the sun."

With a smile, Errante shrugged. "You were probably simply unaware of it. Are you aware of breathing, or the way the oxygen enriches your blood, carrying energy to your cells? Or have you ever focused on how your body processes food to nourish you? It is an instinct, Rafael. You did it without ever thinking about it, like many plants will turn their leaves to follow the sun across the sky, without a single conscious thought."

The thought amused Rafe. "So I'm a plant?"

That earned him one of Errante's rare laughs. The sound was rich and warm, and it flowed over Rafe, more invigorating than the moonlight. Errante was still touching him, and in that moment, Rafe noticed, for the first time, that the moonlight didn't reflect from Errante as it did from everything around them. Errante stood almost as a shadow in the glimmer that bounced from the tents and the reflections that played from the rides and metal enclosures of the concessions. He seemed to absorb the moonlight, and as Rafe looked further, he could almost see the magic around Errante increasing in the soft light.

"If I'm the sun, you're the moon," Rafe said softly, his senses dazzled by the sight. He could feel the edges of his own magic reaching out, merging with Errante's, almost as if they were being drawn together. Silver and gold melting into one another as though longing to become one. As Rafe had been longing for years. It felt as though something between them was connecting, as though they and their magics belonged together.

With a start, Errante pulled his hand away, but Rafe's hand flashed out and he grabbed Errante's wrist. "No, don't. Please," he said, hearing the note of raw appeal in his own voice. He wasn't even sure what he was asking for, really. He just knew he didn't want this to end yet. He wanted more.

Their eyes were locked, and in Errante's, Rafe once again saw the universe. He wasn't even aware of stepping closer until he felt the warmth of their bodies overlapping in the same way as their magic. They were close to the same height, so it was easy for Rafe to lift his free hand and press it against Errante's cheek. Around them all was silent, as though they were enclosed in a cocoon of solitude where only the two of them existed. The light in Errante's eyes changed, shifted, becoming only a single point, which gleamed like molten silver. This time it was Errante who shifted closer, and Rafe's breath caught, as Errante leaned in, closing his eyes and pressing his lips to Rafe's.

How long had Rafe yearned for this? And now, by some

miracle, it was happening. Errante's lips were firm yet soft, and Rafe's own eyes slid closed, the better for him to savor the sensation.

Now that Errante seemed in no danger of pulling away, Rafe released his wrist, only to wrap his arm around Errante and pull him closer. The reality of holding Errante was even better than he'd imagined. They fit together as though they'd been made for one another, and the feeling of Errante's strong, slender body against his made Rafe burn in a way that had nothing to do with magic. Or maybe it had everything to do with magic, only a kind they generated just between the two of them.

He felt Errante's arms slide around his waist, and he gave a small growl of satisfaction. Errante answered the sound with a moan, parting his lips and deepening the kiss. Rafe didn't hesitate to take the invitation, exploring Errante's mouth with a hunger stronger than any he'd ever experienced. Errante tasted of cinnamon and some other spice Rafe couldn't name, but it made him ache for more. Tongues entwined, neither dueling for dominance but giving and taking in equal measure. Someone gave a groan, but Rafe was sure if he'd made the sound or Errante had.

He could feel his arousal growing stronger, the constraint of his clothing against his cock becoming a sort of pleasurable torment. The sensation became almost painful as Errante moved against him, and he could feel hardness sliding against hardness, the inadequate friction just enough to inflame but far from enough to satisfy. He wanted more; he wanted everything, to finally have Errante all for himself, and to give himself in return.

Their magics swirled and combined, adding to the sensation that they were fusing together. Behind Rafe's eyes it was like a shifting pattern, mirroring the kiss and the slow, erotic movements of their bodies. Then there came a surge of power, a feeling of motion, and, startled, Rafe drew back, breaking the kiss as Errante gave a sound of protest. He saw they were now in his own quarters, and somewhere along the way, their clothing had disappeared.

"Wha—" he began in surprise, but Errante put his fingers against Rafe's lips and shook his head.

"If you desire this, desire *me*, do not speak or I shall come to my senses," he said huskily. Errante's accent, one unlike anything Rafe had heard elsewhere, had always been sexy; to hear him speaking of desire in that breathless way was an active assault on Rafe's libido. But Rafe needed no words; he would speak with his body, his lips and tongue and hands, eager to worship Errante's body in any way he could.

Capturing Errante's lips once more, he pulled Errante toward his bed, wrapping his arms around him and tumbling them both onto the soft surface. He rolled until Errante was beneath him, pressing him down into the mattress. Then he began a full assault on Errante's body, wanting to overwhelm him with so much pleasure that Errante would never return to his senses again.

He lifted his head, staring down at Errante, devouring the sight of him in the lights that shone in through the window. As it wasn't moonlight, he could make out highlight and shadow, even see the way Errante's skin was growing flushed and damp with mounting desire. Errante's eyes still contained the silvery glow, but Rafe didn't tell him how utterly beautiful he was. Instead, Rafe lowered his head once more, mouthing kisses over Errante's throat, moving to the side of his neck. There he bit down, making a mark on Errante's smooth skin.

Errante cried out, burying his hands in Rafe's hair, throwing his head back and offering himself up with wanton abandon. This was not the restrained, formal man Rafe had known his entire life; Errante was like an elemental spirit, wild in Rafe's arms. And while Rafe was the mage who manipulated fire, he somehow felt that Errante would be the one to consume him completely.

He continued his exploration of Errante's body, licking, nipping his way downward, dipping his tongue into the hollow at the base of Errante's throat. Then he moved lower, capturing the hard nub of one of Errante's nipples between his teeth, tugging at it as Errante moaned, his hands fisting in Rafe's hair but not pulling him away. Rafe continued on, moving downward, then lifting so he could feast his eyes on the sight of Errante's hard, smooth cock. It was flushed, the head gleaming, and was just as long and elegant as the rest of Errante's body. He glanced upward, finding Errante looking at him, eyes half-lidded and full of desire. Rafe smiled, then held Errante's eyes as he took Errante's cock into his mouth.

With another cry, some word in a language Rafe didn't understand, Errante almost arched off the bed. Rafe gripped his hips, pressing them down into the mattress, squeezing tightly in an obvious command for Errante to be still. To his surprise, Errante did, though his body trembled in reaction, and his breathing was shallow and fast. Rafe could feel Errante's skin growing warm and damp beneath his hands, and he felt a surge of an almost primitive satisfaction. Errante was old and powerful. He'd been to more places and witnessed more things than Rafe could even imagine. But here, in this moment, he was a slave to his own desire and to Rafe's will, and that knowledge alone was headier than the most potent wine.

He took Errante in deeply, then slowly, so slowly, moved his head up again, releasing him bit by tortuous bit. Then he repeated the motion, tormenting Errante, enjoying the inarticulate way he moaned as Rafe tried his best to drive him mad with pleasure. Yet Rafe's own desire was mounting swiftly as well, and as Errante's fingers splayed against his head, he quickened the pace, still drinking in Errante's shadowed expressions and reveling in the mingled scents of sandalwood and desire that rose from his lover's skin.

"Please."

The sound was so soft that Rafe wasn't certain he'd heard it, but then it came again. "Please, Rafael... I burn... I *need*..." Errante moaned the last word in a sound just short of agony, and Rafe at once released his grip on Errante's hips. Gasping, Errante moved, his hands still buried in Rafe's hair as he wantonly fucked Rafe's mouth. Rafe could hear him panting, the thrusts of his hips driving his cock into Rafe's mouth. Rafe moaned, loving every moment, fiercely pleased to be the one who could give this to Errante, who could see past the facade he presented to everyone else to the naked desire now present on his face.

As though Rafe's moan had triggered something, Errante thrust one last time, shattering with a ragged gasp, his seed spilling hotly into Rafe's mouth as Rafe swallowed eagerly, wanting to draw out Errante's release for as long as he could. But finally Errante moaned, his hips falling to the mattress, his fingers unclenching from Rafe's hair. Rafe allowed Errante's cock to slip from his lips, but he lowered his head to Errante's thigh, nuzzling against it like a pampered cat.

For several long moments, the only movement was the stroking of Errante's gentle fingers through Rafe's hair. Rafe could hear the way Errante's breathing slowed, the pulse beneath Rafe's cheek no longer pounding like a drum but easing back to a more normal rhythm. Desire still coursed through Rafe's body, his arousal hard and leaking, but he still didn't move, not wanting to break the magic spell that surrounded them by doing or saying the wrong thing.

Then Errante's hands were on him, urging him up. Thinking that Errante simply wanted to hold him — or be held — Rafe slid upward, completely willing to follow

Errante's lead. He moved into Errante's arms, but as he did so, Errante rolled them both over, until he knelt above Rafe, his knees on either side of Rafe's hips. Bending down, Errante kissed him, pressing their lips together, his tongue sliding into Rafe's mouth and coaxing a moan from him.

Errante's fingers slid up his body, exploring and teasing. He circled Rafe's nipples, coming closer and closer but not touching directly, until Rafe's skin broke out in bumps and a shiver ran over his entire body. Only then did Errante relent, pinching the sensitive nubs between thumb and forefinger. Rafe's groan of pleasure was swallowed into the fusion of their mouths.

A warm pressure flowed over his body with a tingle of some magic he didn't recognize, but must have come from Errante. It made every inch of his skin come to life, as though Errante were stroking him everywhere at the same time. The sensation was so intense, so pleasurable, that he thought he might lose control completely, and he didn't want that. He wanted more; he wanted to know all of Errante and give all of himself in return.

The intense feeling ebbed away, and Errante removed his hands from their pleasurable assault on Rafe's chest. Errante lifted his hips, reaching between their bodies with one hand and wrapping his fingers around Rafe's cock. Before Rafe could even react, Errante moved down, and Rafe felt his cock engulfed in the tight heat of Errante's body.

He hadn't expected this, and his eyes flew open as he gasped, pulling back from their kiss to look up at Errante, feeling a burst of love even more intense than the pleasure Errante gave him. This, *this* was what he wanted, what he had yearned for, dreamed of for all these years. For them to be joined, to feel Errante surrounding him and taking every-thing that Rafe had longed to give him. It was no longer simply sex, it was a joining, two halves finding the whole they could make only together.

Magic tingled over him again, but nothing could compare with the way this felt. Errante was looking down at him, and Rafe saw the way his skin glowed, as though the inner light of his eyes was shining now throughout his body. He was wild and beautiful and somehow free.

Rafe drank in the sight until the demands of his own body to *move* became too much to bear. With a moan, he grasped Errante's hips, moving his own, thrusting upward to seat himself even deeper. Errante braced himself, leaning over Rafe, moving with him as though they had done this before, instinctively seeming to know what Rafe wanted, what he *needed*. There was no sound in the darkened room except the ones made as their bodies danced together, the sounds of their breathing, and the beating of their hearts.

The pleasure in Rafe's body mounted swiftly, more intense than anything in his experience. But still they thrust together, and Rafe could see that Errante was aroused once more, his cock hard and long. He moved one hand from Errante's hip, wrapping his fingers around that proud length and stroking in time to their joining.

Errante threw his head back, arching as he rode Rafe's body, and the glow from his skin strengthened to light the entire room. Rafe distantly noticed that his own skin shimmered gold, but then he was swept up, the sensations becoming almost too much to bear. Rafe thrust once more, lifting his hips from the mattress as he arched up, overwhelmed as his body seemed to burst apart in the most intense pleasure he had ever known. Errante cried out with him, and Rafe hovered there, out of his body yet connected to it, feeling Errante, body and magic and soul, as they truly became one. They were enveloped in light, and Rafe wanted nothing more than to remain this way forever.

Unfortunately his wish was denied, but the return to his body wasn't a loss, because Errante was there, his weight on Rafe's chest, their warm, damp skin pressed together as they breathed in unison. Rafe was happier than he'd ever imagined possible, feeling more alive and yet more drained than he'd thought possible. He barely summoned up the strength to wrap his arms around Errante before a warm darkness replaced the light, and he slept.

CHAPTER 8

Troubled, Errante gazed at Rafe's sleeping form and wondered if he'd killed them both.

He hadn't meant for it to happen. Loving Rafe silently had been difficult, but still safe. It made no waves, raised no questions, and brought no attention. He thought he'd be able to hide it forever — well, hide it from everyone except Persephone — but he'd only been fooling himself. He'd been able to deny himself what he desired, but he'd been completely unable to deny Rafe's need.

If the signs had been there, he'd been blind to them, or perhaps that was simply another bit of self-deception. Hadn't he avoided being alone too much with Rafe ever since he'd realized his own feelings? And he could have had Nik teach Rafe to use his magic, but he hadn't. Perhaps he'd been courting this ever since he'd learned that Persephone knew of his feelings. He couldn't deny that a part of him had wanted this, almost more than he'd wanted to continue living. Rafe loved him, and after the way they'd come together, neither of them could deny what lay between them.

And now Rafe might pay the price.

He closed his eyes, trying to still his mind so he could determine what Path he should now take. His own had always been a mystery, even to himself — it was why he followed others and let them determine his course.

But instead of the emptiness he sought, he found a memory dredged up from a past so long ago that entire civilizations had risen and fallen in the interim.

Brilliant sunlight streamed into a room whose gracefully slender pillars and ornately painted stone walls gleamed with reflected gold. Gossamer curtains of the palest linen fluttered in the breeze from the river, carrying the songs of the boatmen as they came and went from the docks below, their barges weighted down with the wealth of kings. A flight of ibis winged by, their harsh calls sounding as they made their way to the banks where they fed among the mud and reeds. As always, the tang of spices filled the air: the richness of garlic and turmeric, the sweetness of fennel and thyme.

All these things were peripheral to his awareness, the familiar background of his childhood. His attention was directed to the room's only other occupant, who lay reclined on a divan of carved ebony imported from the west. Her dark eyes held his, full of love, and she reached for his hand.

"Do not look at me so, my son," she said in the liquid tones of the language of his birth. Her fingers gripped his firmly as he knelt on the cushion beside her. "This is decided. Your father and I discussed it, and the others agree. Surely from your Travels you must have known this was coming? It is what we must do."

"But you could Travel with me!" he protested, squeezing her hand in return. He felt confusion and even anger. "I am a man now, not a child. You and father would be safe with me. I can Travel to where we would never be found!"

"I wish that were true, ibib, and that we could go with you and see the wonders you will see. But we can't." Her dark gaze was full of sadness. She moved her free hand to stroke his cheek with affec-

tion. *"You still have much to learn, but the time for your father and I is growing short. Our enemy has turned his attention from our cousins, and now seeks to add our power to his. But as cunning as he is, we have a few tricks of our own."*

He would have protested, but he was suddenly held immobile as her magic, so strong and loving, enveloped him. But it didn't simply embrace him as it had in the past, when he'd been barely able to walk and he didn't know his own magic. This time it pushed through his own abilities, stabbing him in the heart, and began to stream into him as though he were a vessel she was filling. Her magic, strong and sure and ancient even by the time he'd been born, poured through him, at first as a trickle, then growing like a wave, for her power was that of the primordial waters. But there was more there, too, other magics he'd felt from his many relatives, each with their own special warmth. He felt the touch of his father's magic, rushing and swirling like the wind. Then followed the temperance and justice of his mother's eldest sister, and the fierce energy of her younger one. There also came the stealthy magic of his father's other wife, who usually kept in the shadows and had rarely spoken to him. He felt the touch of other cousins, and with their magic came their love, and most of all, their hope.

Then the flood ended, and his mother collapsed back on the divan. Her hair, which had been glossy black only moments before, was now the color of an ibis feather. Her smooth skin had grown pinched and wrinkled, and the flesh around her eyes sagged.

He stared at her, horrified at what she had done, sacrificing herself this way. But within him the magic sang, no longer a lake or even an ocean, but a river, as broad and strong and constant as the Nile in flood.

"Why?" he asked, still clutching her hand. "Why do you do this, all of you? To fight him? Do you believe I can defeat him?"

"No, my best beloved," she said, smiling at him even as her eyes grew dimmer. "You are the only one who can escape him. Until now, your Travels have been limited to our home. As he is limited

here, for now, but soon will not be. You can now flee to the stars, and he will never have what he seeks. You are the only one who can do this, my son. You are our last hope."

"But..." he shook his head, confusion warring with the power that still surged and moved inside of him. There was also a rising panic. "I do not know where to go! This is my home, and all I have known. I cannot see my own Path to escape!"

"You must learn, ibib." She raised a hand weakly, in a beckoning gesture. A young woman, no older than he himself, stepped away from the wall where she had stood, hidden in shadows. But he could see her now, could see her Path, and his eyes grew wide as he saw it led to a place he'd never dared go.

"Help her, my son," his mother said, pointing to the young woman. "She has a destiny as well, but it lies far from here. For the sake of Ra and all the rest of us, take her to where she will be safe, but you must not remain. You must Travel, my best beloved. Help those you can along the way, let their Paths guide you to your own. Just know that one day he might find you, and then you must be ready to fight. Oh, beloved, fight him, for his evil will taint not only our world, but all. Your father and his brothers will hold him for as long as they can, but it is simply a distraction to give you time. Fly, my hawk, fly far and fast. It may take centuries, but you will find your own love along the way... do not deny it when it comes. That is my final gift to you, my son. The knowledge that no matter if all of us are gone, you will not have to face him alone."

The light finally fled from her eyes, and her body, now only a vessel, lay still. He felt the tears running down his cheeks, but he ignored them. There would be time for grief later, when he was alone and could give it voice. For now, however, he could not waste this last gift his parents had given him.

He gently put his mother's hand on her chest, then rose to his feet. He looked around the room, at the home he'd grown up in, so familiar and cherished because of the love of his family. Even if he could not see his Path, his mother had set his feet upon it.

Turning to the young woman, who stood with her head bowed in submission, he held out a hand. She looked up with eyes as dark as his own and wide with fear. But he summoned up a smile from somewhere. "Come," he said. "We must leave. What is your name?"

"Neith," she said. "My lord."

He nodded. "Give me your hand, Neith, and close your eyes. We must Travel now... and we will not be coming back."

She did so, and he called her Path, seeing it stretching out into the stars. He'd never ventured beyond the world he knew, but now he must go there, trusting in his new powers to guide him.

Inhaling a deep breath, he took a step.

On the bed, Rafe moved, murmuring in his sleep and throwing out a seeking hand. Errante's heart twisted. He could leave Rafe here, move the Carnival, and perhaps Rafe would be safe. But as soon as the thought occurred to him, he knew he could never do it. He loved Rafe too much, needed him as much as he needed the light of the moon or the air that he breathed. He would have to tell Rafe everything, let Rafe into his confidence, let him closer than anyone had ever been to the truth before.

But not yet. Not until Rafe was stronger. For he saw in their joining that Rafe's magic was greater than he had ever imagined, but Rafe's mind was still that of a man. Putting too much on him at once might cause him to snap and break, like a brittle reed, rather than bending and flexing and returning to stand tall. Rafe had power, but was still fragile. He must be given a chance to grow. If his Fate was to stand by Errante, to fight Errante's enemy at his side, he needed time.

"Errante?"

Rafe's voice was raspy with sleep, but Errante saw the gleam of his heavy-lidded eyes searching for him in the dark room.

"I am here," he replied, then rose to his feet. He crossed

the few feet from the chair to the bed, then sat down on the edge. He took the hand that Rafe held out to him, clasping it.

"Don't leave," Rafe whispered. His eyes opened wider. "What were you doing?"

"Thinking," Errante admitted. "Of you. Of us."

Rafe's fingers tightened on his, and Errante saw the fear in his eyes. "What were you thinking?" he asked.

"Nothing that cannot wait until tomorrow." With that, he slid into the bed, moving closer to Rafe and resting his head on Rafe's broad shoulder. "We shall speak, but not until tomorrow. By morning we must Travel, but tonight, what is left of it, is for us alone."

Rafe grew still, but then he turned his head and captured Errante's lips with his own. Errante sighed, moving into the kiss, closing his eyes, letting himself become lost in the touch of their lips, lost in Rafe. For tonight, the universe could go on without him.

But now he knew that he, himself, could never go on without Rafe. No matter what it cost.

CHAPTER 9

*W*aking up was a slow process, the transition to consciousness taking longer than it usually did. Rafe felt drained, but in a good way, as though all the tension he'd ever felt had left him and now his body was just limp with satiation. He moved his hand, wanting Errante's touch, wanting to see when his lover's beautiful eyes opened.

But the other side of the bed was empty, the sheets cold. Rafe sat up abruptly, looking around the room as he wondered if Errante had woken again and left the bed. But the chair where he'd been the night before was vacant, and Rafe sensed the emptiness of his quarters. No, Errante was gone.

He wondered for a moment if he'd dreamed the entire night, his wishful thinking producing a fantasy so detailed and erotic that his body tightened just thinking about it. But a glance at the pillow beside him showed the indentation where Errante's head had rested, and when he drew in a breath, he caught the scent of sandalwood. No, it had not been a dream that they'd spent the night together, pleasuring one another for hours. It hadn't been just a dream that

Errante had whispered words to him in a language Rafe didn't know, but that he instinctively recognized as a vow of love.

Throwing back the covers, he stood, intending to search for Errante and find out what had gone wrong. Had he done something, said something in the heat of passion that had caused Errante to leave? His heart pounded wildly as he searched for his clothing, before he remembered that Errante had somehow gotten rid of it in the movement between the Midway and Rafe's quarters. He moved to his dresser, intending to grab new ones, when he saw a note lying on top of the oilskin-wrapped book he'd bought weeks ago and hadn't had time to read: a note written in a meticulously precise script.

Rafael —
I promised we would talk, and we shall. Please know that I did not wish to leave you, but I needed to move the Carnival, and you were exhausted and needed your rest. Seek me out when you awaken, but please be discreet. There are reasons for this, which I shall explain.
Know that my heart is still with you, no matter where I am.
— Errante

Rafe's knees went weak with relief, and he dropped into the chair where Errante had been. He'd worried that Errante would deny what had happened, but apparently he wasn't going to do so after all. Then it occurred to him that Errante wouldn't even *have* to deny anything — with his power, he could have made Rafe believe it had simply been a dream, or even erased the memory entirely. But he hadn't, so Rafe had to trust that Errante requested discretion for a valid reason.

It hurt, if he was honest. He would have loved to dash out of his trailer and shout to the entire Carnival that Errante

Ame was *his*. He could imagine the shock of their friends, but he also thought that everyone would be happy for them. Tia Gallier, especially, had been after Rafe for years to "find someone to share all that energy with", and had even cast an eye at Samson when she said it. But she was a loving person who would probably start dropping hints about a wedding as soon as she heard.

But Errante had trusted him enough — and he knew well that his lover wasn't exactly the trusting sort — that he would respect the request. Being able to think of Errante as "his lover" was enough to wipe away the hurt, and cause Rafe to spring to his feet. The sun was up, shining through the windows, and he could actually feel its energy recharging him, far stronger than had the moonlight. All the suns on the all the worlds they'd visited were similar, yet different, but the light here was warm and yellow and beckoned him out of his trailer.

Dressing took only a few moments, and he slid on the familiar weight of the red coat before heading toward the door. Outside, the sunlight beat down strongly, and he raised his face toward it, its power now flooding into him until he felt full of energy. He'd never really sensed it happening before, but now that he knew where his power came from, he embraced the feeling and even reveled in it for a few moments. Perhaps he *was* rather like a plant, as he'd teased Errante the previous day.

As he moved toward the Midway, he nodded greetings to everyone who called out to him, but he didn't stop to talk to anyone. All he could think about was finding Errante and discovering what Errante wanted to tell him.

He reached the Midway, where roustabouts were engaged in some activity at the carousel that Nik had apparently determined was necessary. Rafe had a greater appreciation for what the taciturn engineer did, now that he was aware it was Nik who powered the lights and rides with his own special magic. It still exhausted him to keep the flames he conjured going for over fifteen minutes, so Nik's power had to be much greater than Rafe's own. Yet his was growing; he felt it, could even sense it now as more than the puddle it had been. Maybe not a pond yet, not quite, but definitely larger. He wondered if making love with Errante had been responsible for some of that increase, since he'd had a glimpse of Errante's true power last night. It had been great enough that Rafe hadn't been able to sense its limits, but he was still new at all this.

Thankfully, Errante didn't seem to care that Rafe's power was so much less than his. He didn't want to end up with some kind of inferiority complex about it.

He drew closer to the ticket booth, and finally spotted Errante, dressed in his typical breeches and boots, his white, full-sleeved shirt and black velvet vest. His hair gleamed like raven feathers in the light, lifting in the slight breeze, and Rafe had to resist the urge to run to him, throw his arms around Errante's slender body and kiss him until they were both desperate. That would hardly count as "discreet", would it? Especially when just the thought of Errante's lips could arouse him.

By the time he reached Errante's side, however, he had himself well in hand. Which was a good thing, since Errante wasn't alone. A tall, slender young woman with chestnut brown hair curling over her shoulders and clear hazel eyes stood before him. She wore a simply cut black dress that had to be too warm, given the heat of the morning, but she bore herself with dignity. There was a small bag in her right hand, and Rafe might have thought she was completely at ease, if he hadn't seen the way she gripped the bag too tightly in her hand, the skin of her knuckles white.

"Good morning," he said, giving her a half bow. He

wanted to slide an arm around Errante's waist, but he refrained.

"Rafael." Errante turned, and his dark eyes were warmer than the sun. He didn't smile, but Rafe fancied he could see it anyway, which made his heart beat faster. "This is Amelia Slade. She wishes to join us."

Rafe raised a brow, then looked at her more closely. It was still early in the morning; the Carnival wasn't even set to open for several hours, and how did she know about it, anyway?

"Oh?" he asked, turning his attention back to Errante, who inclined his head.

"She remembers you, but I doubt you remember her, as she was just a child when last we came through this area."

"I do remember you," she said, smiling shyly. She raised her left hand, showing him one of the tokens he gave to children who had been especially good. "I was here with my grandmother, and you were kind to me. You taught me about traveling."

"I did?" The words were out before Rafe could stop them, and then he smiled apologetically. Thinking back, he remembered a little girl from a few weeks previously. This young woman was at least fifteen years older, but it really didn't surprise him. As Errante had said more than once, the Carnival moved in mysterious ways.

"Actually, I do remember you, now that I think back," he said. "You told me that the person you loved most in the world was your mother."

Her face lit up with a sweet smile. "I did! I'm surprised you recall that, after so many years!" She shook her head. "A child's memory is a funny thing, isn't it? You don't look any older to me than you did that day, but you must have been barely a teenager, since it's been fifteen years." She glanced around. "It's funny how the whole place seems exactly the same as my memory of it. Like nothing has really changed."

"Very little changes in the Carnival," Rafe replied. He shot Errante an inquiring glance, since she obviously thought they were nothing more than a simple traveling show. "Are you sure you want to give up your life here and move around with us?"

"I've dreamed of little else since my first visit here," she replied. Her gaze moved to the Big Top. "There's something magical about this place, and I... well. I remember it well and always wanted you to come back so I could go with you."

"I believe Persephone has need of an assistant," Errante said easily. "Your Path has brought you here, so you obviously belong here." He looked at Rafe. "Would you mind taking her to Persephone's tent? She will know what to do. Unfortunately, Nik has urgent need of my attention for a few minutes, or I would conduct Amelia to her myself." He gave a half-bow in her direction. "Rafael is our Ringmaster, and knows almost as much of the Carnival as I, so I'm sure he can answer your questions. If you both will excuse me?"

Rafe bit down on a sigh of frustration, since it meant their talk would be delayed. But he nodded in agreement, then held out an arm to Amelia. "If you will join me, we'll go find Persephone."

There were dimples in her cheeks as she took his arm, trying to look grown up about it, though he could see she was still that same, thoughtful child he'd met such a short time ago. Errante vanished in the way he was capable of, so Rafe started down the Midway toward Persephone's tent.

"He hasn't changed, either," she said. "I mean, Mr. Ame. Is he a magician, the way he's always disappearing?"

"Something like that," Rafe replied easily, then shook his head with a snort. "I think he just likes to keep people guessing."

"Honestly, he's a bit intimidating." She dropped her voice confidentially. "I swear I felt like he could look right through me. It reminded me of a former teacher of mine. We never got away with anything in his class. He always seemed to know when we were up to something."

Having never seen a normal classroom — though he'd read about them — Rafe simply smiled. "You'll find there are many people in the Carnival who are rather surprising," he admitted. "You get used to it."

"Really?" She looked up at him, dimpling again. "You speak from such vast experience?"

He laughed. "I've been in the Carnival almost my entire life. My adoptive mother used to be one of the acts, The Tattooed Lady. She could see right through people as well. I never got away with anything as a boy." Of course, Calliope's tattoos had always betrayed him when he'd tried to fib to her, but that wasn't something young Amelia needed to know. "Ah, here we are. Madame Persephone will teach you a great deal."

The flap of the purple tent was tied open, and Persephone was inside, sitting behind her table with a tarot spread in front of her. Rafe was never sure if she actually needed the cards, or if they were something there as reassurance for the people who sought her advice.

"Welcome, Amelia," she said, smiling at the young woman. Her current appearance, with her long dark hair covered by a filmy veil of purple, seemed little older than Amelia's. "I have been expecting you."

"You have?" Rafe saw the young woman's eyes widen. "Me?"

"Indeed. Please come, have a seat, and we'll have a chat about everything. I've known you were coming for quite some time."

"I'll leave you to your discussion, ladies," Rafe said, giving a slight bow.

Amelia had started toward the table, but she stopped, turning to look at him. "I'll see you again, won't I?" she asked.

"If you become part of the Carnival, you'll hardly be able to avoid me," he replied with a smile. "If you'll excuse me, Errante has something he wanted to discuss with me."

"Indeed," Persephone said, looking at him blandly. "You and I will talk soon as well."

With those cryptic words, she waved him toward the door, so he turned and left. Persephone was one of Errante's closest confidantes — perhaps his only one, come to think of it — so if she saw anything of what they'd been doing last night, no doubt she wanted to make sure his intentions were noble or something. But as he stepped into the sunlight, he dismissed both Persephone and the potential new carnie from his mind, heading back toward the carousel to find Errante.

He didn't see Errante along the Midway, so he slipped between the Big Top and the Carousel. There he saw his lover in a discussion with Nik, frowning in concentration at what the engineer was telling him. But when he saw Rafe, Errante smiled crookedly.

"We are nearly finished here," he said. "Nik was simply telling me that the capacitor for the Carousel discharged, and he needs my help recharging it." He pointed to a very large tube of metal.

"It requires a lot of energy," Nik said, in his softly accented voice. He was as tall and slender as Errante, and handsome, though he didn't have Errante's level of charisma. "Sometimes when we move places, the capacitor drains, depending on the amount of magic in the area." He patted it fondly.

Rafe nodded, though he wasn't an expert by any means.

"So are these how you keep the Carnival powered?" he asked Nik.

"Yes. I can channel energy, but sometimes I need a boost. Charging this myself would take too much time, with the Carnival opening soon."

Errante reached out a hand, and while nothing seemed to happen, Rafe could almost feel the hum in the air around the capacitor. "There, that should do it. Please let me know if any others need it."

"*Hvala*, Errante," Nik replied. "Now I need to get those roustabouts back to work." With a nod, he patted the capacitor again, then headed toward the front of the Carousel.

"Are you free to talk now?" Rafe asked softly. "We have about half an hour before opening."

"Yes," Errante motioned him to follow, then made his way toward his office, which was closer than Rafe's quarters. Rafe had never noticed a bedroom as part of Errante's private space, but, unfortunately, there wasn't enough time to do much of anything if they were actually going to talk.

Once they were inside, however, and the door shut behind them, Rafe moved up to Errante and took him by the shoulders. "I've been discreet, as you requested," he said. "Don't I deserve a reward for obeying without voicing the million questions I have?"

"Indeed," Errante said softly. "But we must talk first."

Sighing, Rafe released him. "All right, then. So what did you need to say?"

Errante put his hands behind his back. "First, I have to tell you that being... involved with me comes with a certain amount of danger."

"From you?" Rafe asked. "Because of all that power you have?"

"Actually, no." Errante frowned. "And yes, but not in the way you think. There is... someone who is after me. He has pursued me since before there even was a Carnival. You have obviously noticed I never leave the magical boundary — it is because I *cannot*. The Carnival is more than just my home — it is my protection. My shield, my disguise. No one can enter it without my knowledge or consent, and that includes my enemy. Therefore, I can never leave it."

A feeling of protective fury arose in Rafe. "Who pursues you, and why? Can we stop them?"

His obvious emotion caused Errante's expression to soften. "I appreciate the thought, but the answer is no. I am safe as long as he never discovers who and where I am. As to who he is… let us call him a cousin of mine. As to why… it is because he is evil and mad for power. He vowed to drain my entire family to fuel his need for conquest, and he did so. Everyone except me."

"You Traveled," Rafe said, immediately understanding. "You could escape. But why…"

Errante held up a hand. "I wanted to bring my family with me. I was… very young. Younger than you are now, in fact, and my power was not as great as it became. But there is a way those of us with magic can transfer it to others. My enemy uses that to *take* the power, but it can also be given, such as I did for you at your first lesson. My parents, my aunts, my stepmother, even some of my cousins, when they saw how powerful our enemy was becoming, knew that there was little they could do against him except fight together. But for each of them he defeated, he would become more powerful, making it harder and harder to stop him. So they each gave up a portion of their power to my mother. She stored it up for a long time, because her well of power was the largest of all. Then, when our enemy grew too close, she poured the stored power, plus all of her own, into me." He dropped his eyes, shivering as though the thought pained him. "In doing so, she began to age and die. But her last words to me were a charge to help others. And to stay ahead of our enemy so that my power would never fall into his hands."

"Oh, Errante." Rafe ached for the sorrow and loneliness in Errante's soft voice, and he longed to pull his lover into his arms, hold him close and never let anything hurt him again. But he sensed Errante needed to get this out, so he settled on all he had: his words. "I'm so sorry."

Errante drew in a deep breath and looked up to meet Rafe's gaze. "It was long, long ago."

"But it still hurts. I can see that." He stepped closer, needing contact as much as Errante seemed to. He took both of Errante's hands in his, hoping to offer some slight comfort.

"It does. It always will," Errante replied softly.

"So, you are telling me that being your lover means your enemy becomes mine?" He considered for a moment. "I'm fine with that. Consider your conscience absolved."

Errante frowned, and he squeezed Rafe's hands almost painfully. "You do not understand, Rafael," he bit out. "He is at least as powerful as I, and… even if I cannot see my Path, even if Persephone cannot determine my Fate, I already know my Destiny. Someday, at a point I do not know and cannot predict, he *will* find me. And when he does, it will be war… and one of us will be destroyed."

"I get it," Rafe said. "It will be a powerful mage battle, and I know I can't fully comprehend what it will be like, because I can't even fully grasp how powerful *you* are. I know I'm young in your eyes. I know I'm just some fire mage who has barely come into his powers, but I don't *care*, don't you see that? If he is your enemy, then he's my enemy, too. I love you, Errante — and no tale of gods and monsters is going to make me feel differently."

For a moment Errante just looked at him, seemed to,

perhaps, look *through* him, but then he smiled slightly. "Thank you. I hope you will think I am worth it in the end."

"You are." Rafe moved one hand to Errante's cheek, stroking it gently. "You're worth everything to me."

"As you are to me." Errante hesitated for a moment. "I love you, too. Those words do not come easily to me — not because I do not feel them, but because I am, deep down, afraid of losing you. Afraid of you suffering at the hands of someone else because of me."

"Then we'll just have to make sure that doesn't happen, right?"

"I have been living the attempt for a long time, and have been successful thus far," Errante told him, his tone a trifle tart. Then he grew more serious. "Unfortunately, I must ask for you to do two things you may find difficult, Rafael."

"Oh?" Rafe tilted his head, curious. "What is that?"

"Please, do not step outside the Carnival. At least… well, at least not until I feel you are powerful enough to protect yourself."

"All right." Rafe didn't mind staying close, if it made Errante feel better. Maybe it would chafe in a few years, but they could address it if that happened. "What is the second thing?"

For a long moment, Errante hesitated. "I love you, but we cannot let our relationship be known to anyone — not even to Persephone or Nik." There must have been something in his expression, because Errante hurried on. "It is not because I am ashamed or worried about what anyone would think. The opinion of others has never been my concern, and I could never be ashamed of how I feel about you. But I worry that if my enemy were to discover my feelings for you, he would come after you. And while I am almost entirely certain he could not get to you inside the Carnival, it is not a risk I am willing to take. I cannot be sure that all the people who come to the Carnival are entirely safe, either. He is known for using trickery, using spies to do his evil bidding. And I *need* you safe, Rafael. I need to know that you will never come to his notice, and that if... if anything were to happen to me, he would never seek you out."

A denial was on Rafe's lips. He *wanted* everyone to know about them, to put his arms around Errante, to kiss him any time he liked. But as he looked into Errante's face, he saw pain and a fear so ancient it was beyond his comprehension. As powerful as Errante was, he believed his enemy to be even more so. If this set Errante's mind at ease, if it made nights like the one just past possible, Rafe would pay the price.

"If that is what you need to feel happy and secure, then I'll do it," he said. "Even though I would prefer to shout my love for you from the center of the Big Top, I'll do it."

"Thank you." Errante leaned into the touch of Rafe's hand on his face. "I hate to ask it. I never thought I would experience the love I feel for you. Perhaps when this is less new, I will feel differently, but for now, I simply must give counsel to my fears for your own safety."

"As long as we can be together, it's a price I'll pay," Rafe replied.

With that, he leaned in and captured Errante's lips with his own. Rafe would stay by Errante's side, no matter what — as ally, as lover, as friend. As long as Errante allowed Rafe to love him, Rafe was willing to face anything for the privilege — even if that meant death itself.

CHAPTER 10

Overhead, the sun shone brightly, making the colors of the Carnival seem even more gay and cheerful. Soon the boisterous crowds would come through the gate, laughing and enjoying the respite that only a show like theirs could offer, when souls were young, and summer was just getting started. The music of the Carousel was jaunty, and the pennants snapped in the light breeze. It was a perfect day.

But Errante's thoughts were troubled.

He walked through the Carnival, head down, thoughts whirling. It was not his normal way, and he caught more than one concerned glance from his small family of performers, though the temporary roustabouts passed him by without notice. He was aware of Samson biting his lip as Errante walked by him, and Darius gave a piteous whine from the front of the next tent. Still, there was a job to do, and the show, as the saying older than Errante's life in the Carnival went, must go on. But it didn't mean he wasn't worried.

It wasn't their current location — the Path to it had been easy, as it lay close to the previous world they'd visited — but what he'd seen on the way there. As he'd stepped through the cosmos, more of a tiptoe in this case, he'd seen the dark spot he'd noticed before. He wasn't certain what it meant, but it had grown larger and more noticeable, though it was still only an insignificant fraction of the multiverse. But it was as though an entire section of the cosmos had either been obscured from his vision — or, even worse, had entirely ceased to be.

He wished he had some idea what it meant, but he didn't, and he feared to Travel in that direction lest he bring himself and the entire Carnival to some horrible fate. It was possible it was his enemy doing it, but if so, that was even more horrifying, since it meant that his pursuer's strength had grown so vast that Errante could never defeat him.

As disturbing as that thought was, Errante was even more troubled by what he feared might be the cause. The only things that had changed recently were his feelings for Rafe, and that they now were lovers. But how could their feelings have possibly precipitated any such thing? It made little sense that Errante could determine, because, even as powerful as he was, he was simply not *that* important in the grand scheme of things.

It had been one of the first lessons his parents taught him, when he'd been young and enchanted with his own abilities — that no matter how important he considered himself to be, there would always be someone greater and more powerful, so he was to be grateful for his magic, and use it to help others; in that way, he might come to expect those more powerful than he to treat him with the same mercy and understanding.

He tried to tell himself it was supremely arrogant to believe that anything occurring in the cosmos had anything to do with him: he was simply a single soul, for all his magic. That whom he loved mattered only to himself, to his beloved, and, unfortunately, probably to his enemy, but not to the universe. And the fact remained that, whatever the cause, *something* was happening that he could not explain. Hence his troubled ruminations.

"A *deben* for your thoughts."

He looked up, finding himself in front of Persephone's tent. She was looking at him with concern, and he sighed. "I should seek your counsel."

She inclined her head, then beckoned him inside. He stepped into the cool shade, immediately struck with the scents of herbs and incense. Amelia, the young woman who had just become Persephone's apprentice, looked up in surprise from where she was lighting candles on a table on one side of the tent.

"Now then, dear, I need to have a bit of a chat with Mr. Ame," she said. "Why don't you take a break and come back in an hour? Everything is ready for opening, so you needn't worry."

"Yes, Madame," she replied. Errante offered her a reassuring smile, to which she gave a somewhat shy curtsey, then left the tent.

"Now then, sit down and tell me what's wrong," she said, indicating a chair on one side of her worktable. When he had, she took the one next to him, not across.

"I am not certain where to begin," he said slowly. While Persephone knew much of his abilities, she didn't know *him*. No one did, not even Rafe, and he intended to keep it that way for their own safety — and, if he were being honest, his own.

"Well, something is bothering you, so start there," she said, raising a brow.

"It has to do with our Travels," he said, wondering how to describe to her something that she'd never experienced. "Recently I have noticed there are areas that are... closed off, perhaps? Inaccessible, or even…" he paused, wondering if he should say the words, but then he reminded himself of all *she* had seen in her life, "possibly destroyed. I have never noticed this before, and while it could have been something I have never paid any attention to, somehow I think… not. And it disturbs me."

She nodded. "Well, I can understand that. Change is difficult," she said, then shook her head. "My friend, I know exactly how you feel. It's like the first time I realized there was someone whose Fate I could not see — I felt as though I'd been punched. I mean, how dare someone be beyond my ken, when I could know the Fates of gods?"

He narrowed his eyes. "You are being ironic, are you not?"

She smiled. "Perhaps a little, but I'm not trying to make light of your feelings. Especially as there is one whom you fear." She looked at him closely. "You believe this has something to do with the Carnival?"

"I do." He sighed, wishing he could tell her of what had changed, but he couldn't take the risk. "Is there anything you think you could discover? Any hints that something wrong is surrounding us?"

"Attempting to read your Fate, or Rafe's, or even my own, is useless, of course," she said. "I could try someone else. Perhaps Nik or one of the Galliers? I've done readings for them before, but it was a long time ago, and they were only interested in the near term."

"Not Nik," Errante said. "He is private, and I have already seen his Path. He will leave the Carnival before too long, as I believe there is something he is called to do elsewhere."

"And not Paul Gallier," Persephone looked at him somberly. "His Fate — well, let us say I would not wish it on anyone Tia Gallier loves."

"Oh?" Even though Errante was aware Paul's Path would lead him away in the not-too-distant future, he didn't know to what purpose. Everyone else's Path kept them with the Carnival indefinitely, but as he'd told the assassin, free will could alter that. Errante was used to the way the Paths of his small family changed, and he knew that, in the fullness of time, everyone would leave to find what they needed elsewhere.

She nodded, then frowned in thought. "Other than me, the person who has been with you longest and who is most likely to remain is Darius."

Errante smiled slightly, despite the seriousness of their conversation. Few people, even those who had been with the Carnival for a long time, knew that Darius was far more than a simple, mixed breed dog who could do all manner of tricks, and bark in a way that seemed to approximate human speech.

"If he is willing, I would be indebted to you both," Errante replied. "If you see nothing out of the ordinary, then there is something going on outside my ability to control. And if you *do* see something… well, perhaps I can change my course, or the course of whatever is causing this."

"Consider it done," Persephone said easily. "I have had no general indications of approaching doom, if that helps set your mind at ease." She placed a comforting hand over his. "You worry, and I understand why. But don't let that worry consume you. I promise if I see doom approaching, I'll tell you at once."

"That helps," he said softly. "I hope you find nothing but happiness for Darius. He's been through enough."

"Indeed." She rose to her feet as Errante did. "I'll let you know when I've spoken to him."

"Thank you." He gave her a courtly bow. "As usual, you have helped to ease my mind."

"Of course," she said, giving him a teasing smile. "It is my job."

He chuckled, gave her another slight bow, and made his way out of the tent. While he didn't have a real answer for what disturbed him – at least not yet – he felt better that Persephone didn't seem worried. If there had been general warnings of approaching disaster, she would have let him know — she had already predicted the end of one world far larger than Errante's small circus.

As he stepped out into the sunlight, he saw Rafe hurrying toward him. His handsome face wore a look of concern, and when he reached Errante, it was easy to see the way he held himself in check from reaching out to touch. It had only been two days since Errante had made his request to keep their relationship private, and Errante could only hope the incredible sex was enough to keep Rafe from regretting their agreement.

"Are you all right?" Rafe asked, keeping his voice low. "Samson said you seemed upset?"

"I am fine," he said, offering a reassuring smile. He had been gone that morning, moving the Carnival while Rafe still slept, so Rafe hadn't seen him since waking. "A minor matter of concern, but Persephone is helping me figure it out. It is nothing that should bother you, I promise. It was an issue of... what was the phrase from that film Mario had everyone watching on the screens some time ago... a disturbance in the force?"

Rafe's expression relaxed a bit. "I see. Are you worried that it's your enemy?"

It was no surprise to Errante that Rafe was so perceptive. "If I am being honest, I was slightly concerned about the possibility," he admitted. "Persephone will do some investigation, as divining the future is more her area than mine. But she does not seem overly concerned, so I am following her lead. And now we have a job to do, do we not?"

"If you need to talk about it, you know I'll listen," Rafe

said. He lifted a hand, placing it on Errante's shoulder, but it was no more than he'd done in the past when they'd spoken. "I may not know who your enemy is, and I don't know if his name would mean nothing to me anyway, right? But if you ever feel the need to confide in someone, to share the burden, I'm here."

Errante was touched, and he laid his hand briefly atop Rafe's, giving it a squeeze before releasing it. "I appreciate the offer, Rafael. Perhaps at some point I shall feel up to sharing the tale, but you need not be concerned about it at the moment. It was long ago, and perhaps I am jumping at shadows."

"All right." Rafe dropped his hand, but he leaned slightly closer. "I look forward to tonight."

Errante felt a shiver run down his spine. His libido, repressed for so long, had woken with a vengeance. It was a wonder that either of them was upright after the last few nights.

"As do I," he said. Then he straightened and looked at Rafe sternly, although he knew his eyes betrayed his amusement. "Now, Ringmaster Harper, I believe you have a show to announce soon, while I must go speak to one of the game handlers. The *Buttons of Mystery* have a part to play here."

"Oh?" Rafe looked interested. "Are you planning on using the cursed painting thing again? That's such a classic, especially when you're trying to bring lovers together."

"Indeed." Errante chuckled. Rafe always made him feel better, and when they were together, he had few doubts. It was only when he was alone that worries seemed to creep in.

Rafe followed Errante back down the Midway. "I hope we can have a magic lesson tonight," he said, even as he tipped his top hat to a lady who was passing by. She giggled, and Rafe smiled. "I want to increase what I can do, so that if anything *does* happen, I can be of help."

"As you wish." He didn't mind; they'd skipped the lessons in favor of spending the time exploring something else that was just as magical, but Rafe was right. They shouldn't neglect his training.

"Until this evening," Rafe gave Errante a courtly bow and a heated look before heading off toward the Big Top. Errante was quite certain Rafe put an extra sway in his step just to torment him — and it was working.

"Errante!"

He turned at the sound of Nik's voice, heading toward the Carousel where the engineer stood, looking perturbed. Nik beckoned him around to the back. "That capacitor drained again; I think I'm going to have to build a new one," he groused, looking at the offending mechanism.

"Is that normal?" Errante asked, frowning in concern. He couldn't remember if Nik had ever had to replace any of his capacitors before, or if it had happened and it had simply slipped his mind. After as long as Errante had lived, he supposed he shouldn't expect himself to recall every minor detail. No doubt he was still a bit on edge from earlier, despite Persephone's reassurances.

"Eventually they wear out, no matter how careful I am. Just a slight overcharge done often enough will burn them out," Nik said. "It's not a major deal, but it means I need a few days. This one is the biggest in the Carnival, and it took me almost a week to build it the first time, if you recall. Can't do it while traveling between places — the magical differentials play havoc with the components until I can get them shielded and sealed."

"We can stay here for several days," Errante said, considering. Normally, he didn't like to spend more than a day or two in one place, lest they attract too much notice from the wrong quarters. This was a magically null world as well, so they stood out even more than normal. But Nik did so much for the Carnival, shouldering much of the day-to-day tasks that needed doing, which freed Errante up to concentrate on the people. "Are you certain you wish to do it, rather than me taking over the Carousel myself?"

Nik smiled. "I would love to have the excuse to get my hands back into constructing something again," he admitted. "As much fun as working with magic is, I rather miss having to do things the hard way sometimes. Used to wrap those copper coils myself by hand."

"If it would amuse you, my friend, we shall take the time," Errante promised. A few days shouldn't matter, and Nik was a good friend who deserved to have a project that fulfilled him.

Nik smiled. "Let me get those no-good roustabouts out directing traffic, and I'll get started at once. Might need you to pull me in a few components as well."

"Just let me know what you need." Errante nodded to him, then headed back toward the Midway.

Perhaps spending a few days in one place would help him get back on an even keel as well. At least it would mean he could wake up next to Rafe in the mornings, rather than having to move the Carnival. A few days of that sounded better than staring at holes in the cosmos and worrying that the end was drawing near. Especially when, thanks to Rafe, it felt like his life was only now truly beginning.

CHAPTER 11

Once he'd left Errante, Rafe headed to the Big Top to make sure everything was in order before the crowds were admitted and the day began. But as he passed by the orange tent used by the clowns, he had the strange sensation that he was being watched. He stopped, turning in place, and at first he saw nothing. But then there was movement, the sway of a dark skirt, and he recognized the form standing in the shadows.

"Amelia? Are you all right?"

The young woman stepped out, and the sunlight caught copper gleams in her hair. She was flushed, and her smile was sheepish.

"Sorry, Ringmaster. I didn't mean to disturb you."

"You aren't," he said, smiling at her. She was so young, and this was probably her first time away from her home and family. "And I'm Rafe, because you are one of us. How are you doing? Settling in? Do you like Madame Persephone?"

"Rafe." She said the word hesitantly, and her blush deepened. But then she rushed on, her eyes shining. "Oh, yes! Madame is amazing! And so reassuring. I was a little confused about what she meant by 'traveling', but… here we are! An entirely different world." She laughed. "When I thought I was joining just a regular traveling carnival, I thought I'd be lucky if we made it to another state!"

Rafe chuckled at her enthusiasm. "I hope that learning that magic was real didn't come as too much of a shock." It usually didn't to those who were destined to Travel with them, but Rafe had never been put in the position of dealing with the sudden knowledge.

"Oh, I've always known magic was real," she said, waving a graceful hand. "I've had visions ever since I was a little girl. My grandma called it 'the Sight.' She said all the women in our family have it. She's the one who said I was destined to go with the carnival when it came back, that I'd find my destiny here. I waited and waited, hoping you would return, and you did!"

The sight of her so enthused warmed Rafe's heart, and he felt another surge of love for Errante. It was all because of him that people like Amelia could find out where they truly belonged. "Well, you're one of our family now," he said. "In fact, you want to know a secret?"

Her eyes grew wide, and she nodded, so he leaned closer. "I knew you were coming back, too."

Her cheeks grew flushed again. "You did?"

"Oh, yes. Mr. Ame said you were special and we'd be seeing you again. I was glad for you, because the Carnival is a wonderful family."

She seemed a little let down. "Oh, I see," she said, then smiled at him again. "Madame said she knew I was coming back, too. But she told me I have a lot to learn, and that magic takes time and practice to develop fully, no matter what talents we are born with."

The words were so close to what Errante had said to *him*

that Rafe laughed. "I was told the same thing only a short while ago."

"You were?" She looked at him in surprise. "But haven't you been here for years?"

"I have, but I also only came into my own magic recently." He sobered a bit; the triggering of his latent abilities was still something that disturbed him, even though it was what had, at last, allowed him to grow closer to Errante as he'd always desired. "I knew I had a little magic, a bit like you and your visions, but I learned a short time ago I have more. And that I have to practice how to use it, and it will take time. So we have something in common."

She smiled, her expression excited. "Perhaps you can give me pointers? I sometimes feel a little awkward asking Madame things that I'm sure she must consider dumb."

"I'm not sure how much help I can give you, to be honest," he said, but held up a hand when her face drooped. "Our magics are very different, since I work with fire. But that doesn't mean you can't talk to me and ask questions if you want to. I suppose that compared to Madame and Mr. Ame, I'm much closer to your age. In fact, I'm far, far closer to your age than Mario is, believe it or not."

"Mario *Gallier*?" She asked, eyes round with surprise. "He's what, perhaps fifteen? Um... I'm twenty-two, and unless you are under thirty, which you can't be if my memory is right..." Her voice trailed off as a question.

The puzzlement on her face was adorable, reminding him so much of the little girl she had been, asking him how her heart could travel. "You have more to learn about the Carnival, I see. Mario is well over one hundred years old in years as you think of them. Perhaps he's closer to two hundred. He remains as he is because it is his wish to do so, and Mr. Ame allows it."

"But..." she shook her head, then laughed. "Magic. Right. I

am definitely getting the idea that I have a *lot* more to learn about my new home. Yet that begs the question about how old *you* are, Mr. Ringmaster Rafe."

"I think around seventy," he admitted, then shrugged. "I was a child here, but Mr. Ame let me grow up, because that's what *I* wanted. My adoptive mother used to keep track of my age for me, but when she moved on to another place, I stopped counting. It doesn't really seem to matter much anymore." And, if he were being honest with himself, he didn't want to think of himself as a literal child when compared to his own lover. That just seemed wrong.

"Wow." She blinked several times, apparently trying to wrap her head around the concept. "So... does that mean I won't..."

"Not if you don't want to age, no. I think that's about the standard, though, so if you *do* want to get older, talk to Mr. Ame," he said. "Otherwise, don't worry about it, right? You're safe here. You can explore your magic and take as long as you need to do it. And it's always interesting to meet new people, don't you think?"

"Yes, I think it would be." She really was still as sharp as she'd been as a child, and it showed flexibility that she seemed able to roll with the revelations. "And Madame says that in a little while, I'll be able to go outside the Carnival and see some of the worlds we visit."

"You will, and it's fun at first," he said. Of course, he'd promised not to leave the Carnival, but he didn't think he'd miss it much. "Make sure you go with some roustabouts, like Simeon or Bill, Bob, and Biff. Or with the Galliers, though they don't leave often. We don't go alone much of anywhere 'outside'. It's just a matter of safety, at least until you've grown enough into your own abilities to protect yourself."

"That makes sense," she said, shrugging slightly. "I mean, even back home, I knew there were places not to go unless someone was with me, and an entirely new world... don't worry. I waited a long time to come with you, and I don't want to do anything stupid to mess that up!"

"Good." He smiled at her, then patted her on the shoulder. "I've enjoyed our chat, but I should go now. I have to check on the Big Top before we open, and I suspect you need to return to Madame, right?"

"I do," she admitted, looking a bit embarrassed. "Thanks for the talk... Rafe."

"Of course," he told her, then gave her a sweeping bow. "You're one of us now, Amelia, and I suspect you'll have a long and happy journey with us. I'll see you later, fair maiden. Adieu!"

She laughed at his nonsense, as he'd hoped she would. It was part of his job to make sure everyone was comfortable and happy at the Carnival, even the people who were part of it. He acknowledged her small curtsey — a gesture she had probably picked up from Persephone — and then turned once again for the Big Top. Amelia would do just fine in the Carnival, and Rafe could make sure that she made some friends her own age.

AFTER THEIR DUTIES for the day were complete, Rafe was eager to meet up with Errante. There was so little time for much interaction with their different schedules, and today had been especially busy. So as he approached the Big Top, Rafe was eager for just the sight of his lover.

But as he slipped through the canvas flap, he found the trapezes still in place, the scents of sawdust and popcorn hanging in the air as they always did after a show. The bleachers were empty, and there wasn't a sign of anyone else.

Since he'd not had time to run back to his quarters, Rafe doffed the red coat and put it on one bleacher, adding his top hat to the pile.

"I am sorry to be late."

Errante's voice came from behind him, and Rafe turned, smiling widely. Errante seemed to take a positive delight in sneaking up on people unawares, which Rafe was pretty certain was less from being stealthy than 'Traveling' a short distance and popping up wherever he liked. He'd asked Errante about it once, many years before, to be met with nothing more than one of Errante's enigmatic smiles and a comment that there were some mysteries Errante preferred to remain his own.

"I understand. It's been a bit more chaotic today than usual, hasn't it?" Rafe replied, stepping closer to Errante. He wanted to pull him into an embrace and steal a kiss, but he'd promised, so he didn't. But he hadn't promised not to stand close enough to feel the heat from Errante's body, and to his relief, Errante didn't step back. Instead, he smiled at Rafe, his expression warm.

"Indeed, it has," he said. "There were more people whose Paths required my attention today than there usually are, as well as Nik needing for me to Travel in some supplies for his new capacitor. But I am here now, so we may begin."

"Don't you ever get fatigued?" Rafe asked, suddenly curious. "I mean, you told me you can recharge from the moonlight, but you never really seem fatigued from all the magic you do to keep the Carnival going. Come to think of it... stepping between worlds must require an incredible amount of magic."

Errante inclined his head. "It has happened, but not for quite some time. Remember, I have had many, many years to build up my magical reservoir. Yours will increase, I have no doubt. I sense there is a depth to yours as yet untapped. And just as your latent abilities manifested, we shall discover what we need for you to access and use your innate strength." He crossed his arms over his chest. "But enough about me — I know how to use my magic. This is your lesson, Rafael. May I assume you have failed to practice the last few days?"

Rafe smiled. "I throw myself on the mercy of my master. I have been rather busy attending to other... needs."

Errante's lips twitched. "Well. May I hope that you at least availed yourself of the sunlight and feel strong enough to continue with your lessons?" At Rafe's nod, he waved a hand, banishing the trappings of the Big Top, and leaving them with a large, open space. "Very well, then. We will continue where we left off. A sphere, if you please. I want you to shrink it down as far as you can. That way I can see not only your control, but how much magic you can exert and for how long."

Rafe conjured the ball of fire, and Errante walked him through the exercise of reducing it in size, while making it stronger and brighter. As he did so, Rafe could feel the power he was drawing from within himself and could even feel that his reservoir was bigger than it had been. He looked at Errante over the brilliant light he held before him, seeing Errante's smile of approval. It made his heart beat faster and called to mind what it was like to make love with him, to feel their magic swirling together.

"Attend, Rafael!" Errante said, and Rafe realized the sphere had expanded again as he grew distracted. He focused once more on the sphere, forcing it down smaller. It drained his magic more quickly, but he kept going. The more he tried to shrink the sphere, the more magic he had to draw. The ball shrank down to the size of one of the ping-pong balls used in the fishbowl game, then down to the size of a marble. At that point, it was glowing white at the edges, while the center had turned nearly blue. When he felt he was almost at the end of his endurance, Errante spoke again.

"Now slowly, slowly let it expand," he directed, his voice soft. Rafe noticed distantly that Errante had his hands raised as well, and the air shimmered between them. "Carefully, please."

Rafe did as he was told and was surprised that it was still draining to keep the sphere expanding slowly. He could feel that it *wanted* to expand because of the entropy, as Errante had explained. He could feel sweat rolling down his face. "Why can't I just let it go?"

"Too quick of a release will cause an explosion," Errante told him. "But I have a shield to encase it, if you cannot manage it. Do you need to let it go?"

"I… I can do it." Rafe never removed his eyes from the sphere, grinding his teeth with the effort of slowing the expansion. Finally, after what felt like an eternity, the sphere had grown to its original size once more, and with a sigh, he let it go, knowing it was no longer dangerous.

By the time the last of the ball dissipated, Rafe sank to the ground. He was soaked in sweat, and his muscles were trembling. He felt drained, and yet elated. He'd done it! Even though he didn't think he had enough left in him to produce even a tiny flame, he knew that his power had grown a great deal from where he'd started.

"Excellent, Rafael," Errante said. He came over and knelt down beside Rafe, not seeming to care that he was going to end up covered in dirt. Errante's smile was fiercely proud. "That was amazing! Perhaps I should have stopped you before you went so far, but you were doing well. I would have allowed nothing to hurt you, or me, or the Carnival. But you did it all on your own."

"I didn't know I had it in me, to be honest," he replied. "Did I really do well?"

"Perfectly. I am very proud of you." Errante reached out to touch his arm. "Just never practice that without me around, if you please. Not until you are much stronger and it does not leave you drained. But for now, you deserve a reward."

Rafe was pleased that Errante was proud of him, but he didn't have the energy to tease, as he normally would. "Not walking back to my quarters would be reward enough. I don't think I have the strength for anything else."

"Oh, I think I can take care of that," Errante replied easily, giving Rafe a heated smile.

And much to the delight of them both, he did.

CHAPTER 12

Golden sunlight peeked around the edges of the curtains, one beam striking Errante's eyes. He cracked them open, finding himself looking over an expanse of lightly furred skin that rose and fell slowly. He smiled, rubbing his cheek against Rafe's chest like a pampered cat. He'd not had the luxury of waking up after spending an entire night in another's arms since he'd left his first life, and that was so long ago that he could barely remember what it felt like. That he was waking up cradled against Rafe's body made it absolutely perfect, the incredible feeling of giving love and being loved in return adding another layer to the joy of their physical union. It made him wish he never had to move again.

He watched the sunlight strike Rafe's skin, making it seem to shimmer. They belonged together. He felt it more and more every time they made love. Two halves of a whole, only made complete when they were together. He supposed their union had been inevitable from the moment Rafe had entered the Carnival, but he was glad it had taken them so long to find their way to one another. It made him feel less worried about the vast difference in their ages, since Rafe had lived enough to know what he wanted, and had visited enough other worlds and met enough people that if he'd felt a pull to anyone else, he could have left of his own free will.

If it weren't for the enemy he knew would never give up pursuit, Errante would have considered his life as close to perfect as it was possible to be. As it was, he would rather focus on the reality of Rafe than on the nebulous danger that had hounded him for longer than he cared to think about.

That brought to mind the power Rafe had exhibited during his lesson the previous night. Errante had been surprised that Rafe had condensed so much power and remained in control of it. If that power had been released, it would have been enough to destroy the Big Top, at the very least, if it weren't for the protective magic Errante had spent hundreds of years constructing around every part of the Carnival. Rafe had drained himself almost completely in the process, and when Errante had replenished him the previous night, he could *feel* how much the reservoir of Rafe's magic had grown. No longer a puddle, or even a lake, it was rapidly expanding toward that potential Errante had first sensed when Rafe's abilities had manifested. Rafe would be incredibly powerful in the future, and Errante knew it would be a power that could raze and destroy. If Rafe could destroy a village as a child, what he could do as a man could likely devastate a continent. It was Errante's duty, and his privilege, he felt, to guide Rafe into learning and controlling his powers. It was a blessing to them both that Rafe's temperament was even and his instincts were those of a protector, rather than a destroyer. Errante had seen what unchecked power could do, and it was up to him to make sure Rafe did nothing with his magic that he would come to regret.

Rafe stirred, cracking one eye open, then smiling sleepily at him. Just the sight of that smile made Errante's heart melt, and he couldn't resist craning up to press their lips together. With a chuckle, Rafe pulled Errante into his arms, their morning erections sliding together so that they both moaned into the kiss. They continued that way for a while, slow and easy, hips moving, tongues entwined, their skin warming as arousal and need grew stronger.

After a time Rafe drew back, pressing kisses over Errante's face before looking into his eyes. "This time, I want you to take *me*," he murmured. "I need to feel you inside me, love. I want to be yours completely."

Errante smiled. Until now Rafe had been the one to do the taking, which Errante enjoyed very much, but he was completely willing to be flexible if Rafe wished it. "You are already mine, as I am yours, but I shall give you anything you desire that is within my power."

Rafe rolled onto his back, pulling Errante with him. Nestling between Rafe's legs, he conjured a handful of lube, then rubbed his hands together. Encircling Rafe's cock with one hand, he gave it a teasing stroke, which caused Rafe to throw his head back on the pillow and groan.

"Tease," Rafe gasped.

"Impatient," Errante responded, then smiled wickedly. "You have not yet seen all I can do to torment you, my Rafael."

He scooted back slightly, then with his free hand, conjured lubrication. He pressed one finger against the puckered opening to Rafe's body, circling slowly, which after several moments caused Rafe to growl and squirm with impatience. He could have used magic for preparation — indeed, that sort of spell was something he'd learned when he'd first learned about sex — but he preferred to draw this out, to pleasure Rafe slowly and drink in the knowledge that it was he who drove Rafe mad.

When Rafe's skin grew flushed and his breathing had

quickened, Errante finally relented and pressed against the pucker, his finger sliding into the tight heat of Rafe's body. He continued the torment that way for a few minutes, as Rafe clutched at the sheets.

"Yes, please, more," Rafe begged, his dark eyes wide with need. "Errante, please…"

There was no way for Errante to deny anything when Rafe begged, and his own arousal was growing so hard, it was almost painful.

"Very well, since you said please," he replied, and added another finger. It was swiftly followed by a third, and Errante pressed in, seeking that sweet spot men had known for even longer than Errante himself had existed.

When he found it, Rafe arched backward on the bed, crying out Errante's name. His cock was leaking, and Errante knew it wouldn't take much to send Rafe soaring over the edge. So when Rafe relaxed back down, panting hard, Errante removed his fingers, then grasped Rafe's hips, rising on his knees. He took a moment to admire Rafe, his skin flushed and damp, eyes begging Errante for fulfillment, and Errante had no desire to deny either of them.

"You are mine, best beloved, heart of my heart," he said, using the tongue of his birth. "Always and forever, until all the suns of the heavens die, and the gods themselves are no more."

He positioned himself, then slowly eased forward, taking his time, savoring the feeling of sheathing himself in Rafe's body, of being welcomed, of being loved and desired beyond measure. When he was seated deeply, Rafe grasped his shoulders.

"Love me," Rafe moaned. "I need you."

Errante braced himself on one arm, then once more wrapped his fingers around Rafe's cock. With that, he began to move, pulling back, then slamming his hips forward to bury himself deeply in Rafe's body once again. With each thrust, Rafe moaned, his fingers tightening on Errante's shoulders, nails digging into his skin. Errante enjoyed the slight prickle of pain, which only fueled his own desire.

"More!" This was not a request, but a demand, and Errante couldn't resist it any more than he'd been able to refuse Rafe's pleas. He moved faster, his own need fueling the pace, and he stroked Rafe in time to the hard thrusts of his hips.

Around them, magic swirled, ebbing and flowing, dancing over their skin in a caress like a warm breeze. It added to the sensation of their joining, something unique to them. Errante's magic had never flowed for any other lover, and the feeling of Rafe's power reaching out and twining with his was a pleasure all its own.

Panting, sweat dappling his skin, Rafe finally cried out, his climax overcoming him in waves of pleasure Errante could feel. Golden light sparkled on his skin and in his eyes. It set Errante off, ecstasy blazing along every nerve in his body as he surged forward one last time, pulsing his release into Rafe's body even as his soul was filled with the warmth of Rafe's spirit. Nothing constrained them, not the walls of the room, not the magic of the Carnival, not even the flesh of their bodies. They were one, for a glorious moment that was forever and yet a time all too brief.

Slowly, slowly they drifted down from the heights, until Errante felt himself weighted down once again, bound to this world and to the mortal needs of his body. Rafe looked at him, lifting a hand to stroke Errante's hair back from his damp face, with a smile so full of love it made Errante's heart swell. How had he managed so many long, lonely years without this?

"What did you say before?" Rafe asked softly. "I heard the

words, but I couldn't understand the language. It was beautiful, though."

"I said that you were mine, and I was yours and always would be," Errante replied. "The language of my birth, which I fear is lost to the sands of time."

"I'm sorry," Rafe cradled Errante's cheek. "Persephone once told me you were the loneliest man she had ever met."

"No longer," Errante moved up, kissing Rafe briefly before laying down once again upon his strong shoulder. "Because of you, my Rafael."

"I'm glad." Rafe sighed, and Errante felt him press a kiss to his hair. "I only want you to be happy."

"As I do you," Errante replied.

They lay still for a few minutes longer, then Errante sighed. "I fear I must go. There are things that the pleasure of your arms tempt me to ignore, but unfortunately, duty calls."

Rafe grumbled, kissed him hard, then released him. "The burdens of being the manager, I suppose. I'm glad I'm only one of the worker bees. That means I can lounge in bed for a while before I have to worry about my own duties."

"You are as spoiled as a temple cat," Errante retorted, but he smiled as he rolled away and rose to his feet. "But unlike the cats, you need a shower, which I will leave you to."

"Oh? And what about you?" Rafe asked, propping himself up on one arm.

He looked so tempting lying there that Errante wanted to rejoin him, but he sighed and shook his head. "While I enjoy indulging in a hedonistic bath, I do not have the time." He gestured, using magic to clean and clothe himself. "Perhaps one day before we leave this world, we will have the time to enjoy a bath together, if you would like."

"I would love it," Rafe replied. "Have you always been hiding a big tub somewhere that I haven't known about?"

"No, but I shall make one just for you." He smiled teasingly. "But I shall leave it to you to keep the water at the perfect temperature for as long as we are in it. It can be another lesson."

That earned him a laugh from Rafe, and Errante leaned down, stealing a final kiss, before turning to Travel from Rafe's quarters. Perhaps, he thought, he could give the entire Carnival a day off while they were waiting for Nik to finish his task. An entire day lounging in a tub with Rafe sounded as close to heaven as he thought he might ever come.

CHAPTER 13

After Errante had left, Rafe had lounged in bed for a time, but he hadn't been able to sleep. Instead, he'd gotten up, taken a long, hot shower, imagining how Errante would look beneath the water, golden skin gleaming, his black hair beaded with water. He hoped they had time for a bath together soon. As luxurious as it had been to spend the entire night together, he wanted even more. He wanted to be by Errante's side every moment of the day, to bask in the love they shared.

Once he left the shower, he dried off and dressed in a clean pair of dark breeches and a fresh white shirt. He slipped on his boots, then looked about, frowning when he couldn't find his red coat. It was the one item of clothing that didn't just appear every morning. It was always where he left it at night, though it never seemed to need cleaning. He'd wondered from time to time if there was something special about the coat, since there was only one of them, and despite it having been worn by every Ringmaster the Carnival had ever had. In every incarnation on every different world, it was still somehow always the same.

He looked around his quarters, then paused, thinking about the night before. Just as he recalled that he'd last removed it in the Big Top, a knock came to his door, and he moved to answer it.

Outside his door stood Amelia, holding his coat and top hat. She looked at him curiously. "Madame told me to bring these to you, Rafe," she said.

"Thank you," he replied, giving a rueful smile. "I only just remembered that I hadn't taken them off here last night. I left them in the Big Top by accident." They'd disappeared when Errante had banished the bleachers, but they must have reappeared when the Big Top had been restored. Rafe had been too weak to have noticed, especially since Errante had banished the rest of their clothing when transporting them to Rafe's quarters. No doubt the coat had slipped Errante's mind as well, but then they'd both been too preoccupied with one another for it to have mattered.

"Oh?" she asked, tilting her head to the side. He could almost read the thought on her face, and he flushed slightly. That was a truth she would not hear from him.

"I had a magic lesson with Mr. Ame last night, and I'd taken them off beforehand," he said quickly. He knew he didn't owe her an explanation, but with the discretion Errante wanted, it was better to make sure no gossip got started than to quell it once it had begun. "I'm still new enough to my powers that I ended up draining myself to the point I could barely walk. Mr. Ame helped me back to my quarters, but I guess he didn't even see the coat."

"Ah..." Apparently the explanation was good enough, since she nodded. Rafe hoped wherever Errante had banished their clothing in transit, it didn't end up being discovered by someone else; there were enough magical beings in the Carnival that if a pair of random boxer briefs turned up, they could be traced back to him — and blaming *that* on a magic lesson would be impossible.

"Well, thank you again," he said. "I guess I should finish getting ready." He pointed to the coat and hat, which she still held.

"Oh!" Her cheeks went pink, and she held out the clothing. "Sorry, I should have…"

She had been handing the clothing to him, and as he took it, their hands brushed together. She stopped speaking, her body suddenly going rigid, and her eyes changing from clear hazel to an opaque, misty white.

"The book," she said, in a strange, hollow tone of voice that made a shiver go down Rafe's spine. It was empty, like the wind if it had a voice. "The book is important. Heed its lessons and you may live. Ignore it at your peril, for you will lose all you love."

As Rafe gaped at her, her eyes cleared, and her body relaxed. She shook her head like a swimmer coming out of water. "Wow, that was a stronger one than usual," she said, pressing a hand to her forehead. "And it *hurt!*"

It took Rafe a moment to gather his wits. "Are you all right?" he asked, stepping forward and taking her arm. He was careful not to touch her bare skin, in case that was what triggered the vision.

"I'll be fine in a moment," she said, then looked up at Rafe with a slight smile. "One thing about my magic, I never know when it's going to hit me. Madame says I just need to learn to summon it when I want it, but it's a little hard to keep it at bay when I *don't* want it."

"I'm so sorry, that sounds annoying," he said. He took his coat, releasing her arm long enough to don it quickly as he kept an eye on her. She seemed to get better, the color slowly returning to her face. As he set the top hat on his head, she gave a shudder and drew a deep breath.

"Okay, better," she said. "The headache didn't last as long this time, thankfully."

"I'm glad, but let me walk you to Madame's tent," he said. He offered her his arm. "Unless you prefer to go without my company."

"I appreciate it a lot," she said, smiling widely as she took his arm. "Usually, I don't get them close together, but I guess there's always a first time."

"True," he replied. He closed the door to his quarters, then they started off toward Persephone's tent. The Carnival was still rather empty at this early hour, though as they passed the Carousel, he heard Errante's distinctive accent as he talked with Nik. A few roustabouts were going about some clean up that had been missed the night before, and a few of the concession stands were just beginning their preparations for the day. Amelia remained quiet at his side, and since she probably still had a bit of a headache, Rafe remained quiet as well.

Then she spoke. Lifting a hand, she gestured around the Carnival. "You know, something just struck me. There are no animal acts, like lions or elephants, not even a snake charmer. I guess there is Darius, but... that's different, isn't it?"

"It is," Rafe replied with a smile. "Darius came of his own free will. He remains and performs because it's his choice. Errante doesn't believe that animals should be used. Even the goldfish in that game—" he pointed to the stand where the fish were, their inhabitants swimming in dreamy circles within their bowls, "—can make the choice of where they wish to go. Errante feels deeply about individuals, no matter how small. In fact, the smaller and more helpless, the more he seems to care about them."

She considered that, then smiled up at him. "That's an enlightened way of looking at it. Back home, there has been a big movement for years to get animals released from things like circuses and aquariums. I guess he's just ahead of his time."

"I grew up here, so it's normal to me," he shrugged. "You will see horses when we go to a world where we can't have the appearance of technology, but they are illusions. Even the birds and rabbits in Mephistopheles' show are nothing more than a very convincing illusion."

"Interesting. I'll have to take a look, since I've not seen the magic show since I arrived." Then she laughed, the sound bright with happiness. "I just realized how that sounds. I mean, the whole place is nothing but one big magic show!"

Rafe laughed with her, thinking back to the way he and Errante had just made love. "It certainly is."

Once they reached Persephone's tent, he held upon the flap for her, and then followed her inside. Persephone, who had been peering at a deck of Tarot cards, didn't even look up at their entrance..

"Another vision, dear?" She asked, flipping over a card. She gave a nod, then finally turned her attention to them, rising to her feet and approaching.

"Yes, Madame," Amelia replied. She had released Rafe's arm when they arrived, and Rafe was glad she seemed to be fine now.

Persephone looked her over, tsking softly. "I'll see if we can set a different set of meditations for you, so that you can control when they come." She glanced at Rafe, raising a brow. "I felt the magic when her vision began. I assume it was in relation to you?"

Rafe nodded, embarrassed, as though it were somehow his fault. "I suppose so. Our hands met when she was handing me the coat, and then she just went stiff and started talking in a very odd voice about paying attention to a book."

"Hmmm." She looked at Amelia again. "It's early, dear

child. You go lie down in the back and take a little rest. There's no reason to push yourself. In fact, if you feel up to it, meditate a bit, and see if you can think of how the vision was triggered — if it was a touch of skin, or of your magic to Rafe's, or even something else unrelated."

"Yes, Madame," Amelia replied. She smiled at Rafe. "Thanks for walking me back."

"Of course. I hope you feel better," he replied. She nodded, then headed back through some draperies at the rear of the tent.

Persephone waved a hand, then turned to him. "She won't be able to hear us now," she said. "So, tell me, how long have you and Errante been lovers? And why wasn't I told?"

Rafe knew he must be staring at her like an idiot, but he couldn't help it. "What? How... Did you *see...?*"

Persephone threw her hands up in the air. "Men! I don't have to be a seeress to use my eyes and ears, child. I had breakfast with Tia Gallier, as I often do. I went out through the Big Top, when I spied your jacket and top hat sitting there plain as can be. I picked them up, intending to return them to you, but as I got close to your quarters, I heard... well. I heard enough to tell you weren't alone, shall we say? Given how you feel about Errante and how *he* feels about *you*, it didn't take me more than a second to put it all together."

Rafe wondered wildly what he could say to convince her that she was wrong. Errante didn't want anyone to know, for reasons that Rafe didn't understand, but which he respected because they were Errante's reasons. "Um... I wasn't alone, but it wasn't..."

He couldn't finish the lie, not in the face of the look she gave him.

"Fine, fine. I see denial isn't simply a river," she said tartly. "But I'll give you my congratulations, anyway. And before you say a word, I know why it was probably Errante who asked you not to tell anyone and why you agreed. Maybe he's right, but maybe he's wrong, too. I just want you both to be happy."

Rafe drew in a breath. "Do you think anyone else knows?" he asked, dropping his voice. He didn't confirm what she believed, so it shouldn't count as telling anyone.

"Unlikely." Persephone shrugged. "Listen, Rafael. I am a student of people's motivations and emotions. Yes, I have a gift of Seeing, but often a person's Fate is so muddied by untaken paths and unresolved traumas that there are too many possible outcomes to choose from. Free will and all that is a bitch, but I know enough of *people* that I can often select the correct outcome just by looking at them. Most people, however, don't look any deeper than the superficial appearance of things. Even for people they have known for years, and who they count as friends. There are secrets to this Carnival that even Errante doesn't know, and I am certain there are things that escape even me, much as I look for the hidden. If you wish things to remain secret, they likely will, at least for a time. *I* certainly won't tell anyone. If the information comes out, it will probably be because one of you wants it to. Otherwise, I don't know why Errante didn't spell your quarters to be as soundproofed as mine."

"I... see." Rafe didn't know how to feel about all that, and he hoped Errante wouldn't be upset that Persephone knew — because he was going to have to tell him, and hope that he could forestall Errante ending things "for his own safety" just as they were getting started.

"You don't, but you will," she reached out to pat his hand. "I'm keeping watch, and while there are things that escape me from time to time, it isn't much nor often. And I want the two of you to be happy."

"I'm trying," Rafe replied with a sigh. "I almost wish you

hadn't said anything about knowing, since that puts me under a bit of strain. I'll have to tell Errante…"

"Tell him. I knew his feelings for you — and yours for him — for years while the two of you danced around one another and cast longing looks from afar." She rolled her eyes, but then smiled at him in a motherly way, patting his hand again. "If it makes you feel better, you can chalk it up to my Sight, or even to it being impossible to hide something from a person who once changed your diapers. Besides, I promised Calliope to keep an eye on you until she comes back."

Rafe smiled crookedly. "Thanks," he murmured, shaking his head. Persephone really was like an aunt or something to him, so if anyone had to know, at least the information was probably safe with her.

"Of course. And as for Amelia's Vision — something about a book? I suggest you go back and worry about that. It seems to be important. Amelia isn't in control of what she Sees or when she Sees it yet, but that doesn't mean it's invalid."

"All right, I will." Rafe nodded, then gave her a slight bow. "I'll do it right now, in fact. Will you excuse me?"

"Go on." She waved a hand at him. "I'll see you both later."

He made his escape, stepping out into the early sunshine and heading back toward his quarters. In order to keep from worrying about what Errante would do or think, he focused instead on Amelia's strange vision.

He had a lot of books, so he wasn't certain which one she was referring to. When he reached his quarters, he headed to his bookshelf, looking at the spines facing him and wondering which one could be so important. He'd read all of them, some of them multiple times, and nothing struck him as being about a subject that would result in something horrible if he didn't "heed" it. He turned away, frowning, wondering if what she'd really meant was that he should go out on *this* world, and there would be a bookshop where he'd find the relevant tome. But that was impossible, since he'd promised Errante he wouldn't set foot outside the Carnival!

Growling in frustration, he went back into his bedroom, intending to tidy up his bed before going out to begin his work for the day. Magic did many things in the Carnival, but he still had to straighten up his own messes, which bothered him not at all. Sometimes setting things in order soothed him when he was feeling unnerved, as he was at the moment.

But when he walked past his dresser, his eyes fell on the oil-skin wrapped package sitting on top of it, almost hidden behind a picture of him and Calliope in an ornate silver frame. It was the book he'd picked up that day when he'd been attacked, and which he'd put out of his mind. He couldn't remember picking it up from the ground before he'd run for the Carnival, but he must have grabbed it and then put it here and forgotten it. Could it be the book of Amelia's vision?

He hesitated, then picked it up warily, turning the package over in his hands. He remembered the odd book-seller, with his blond ringlets and kind eyes, and the magic he'd felt coming from the shopkeeper. Rafe hadn't even selected this book himself. He'd been more or less bidden to take it, so off-kilter from the strange encounter that he hadn't resisted. He couldn't even remember what the book was supposed to be about.

He untied the leather ribbon holding it closed, then peeled back the oilskin which had protected it from the mist that day. He dropped it on the floor, unheeded, and let the inner paper layer follow it. He turned the book upright in his hands, regarding the cover and its gold embossed title.

What in the multiverse was an *Ancient Egypt*?

Opening the book to the beginning, he scanned the first few pages, which described excavations that had taken place "recently" — whatever *that* meant given he had no frame of reference — in the "Necropolis of Karnak." Ah, that meant Egypt was a place, so that was one mystery solved at least. The place was in a desert along a great river called the Nile.

Abruptly he remembered something Persephone had said only a few minutes before: "Denial isn't simply a river." He'd heard her say it how many times over the years? He'd thought it was just some odd saying, and he'd never heard anyone else use it. Was this a book about Persephone's world of origin?

He sat down on the edge of the bed and skimmed over several more pages that described the unearthing of a funerary complex and the process of exposing and cleaning a temple that had lain buried for four thousand years. The archeologists had taken great pains to copy down the engravings on the temple, then sent them to London — and *that* name he recognized from Simeon, even if he remembered little about the place from the Carnival's visit there — to be translated. The rest of the book claimed to contain legends from the temple of the Goddess Mut, one of the greatest goddesses of the land.

Rafael still didn't know what he was supposed to glean from the information, but his fascination grew as he read of how Mut gave birth to the world in primordial waters before marrying Amun, a god of the air and sky. They had one child, named Khonsu, who was the god of the moon. A god whose name meant "Traveler."

Rafe stopped, a prickle of gooseflesh breaking out on his skin. Then he forced his eyes to continue along the page. Khonsu seemed to be a life-giving god, who protected and aided those who traveled. He read how Khonsu had various titles, like 'Defender', 'Embracer', 'Healer'... and *Pathfinder*.

At that moment, he knew the truth. Errante, his lover, who helped people, protected them, who even said he could see their Path, was much, much more than he seemed. He was more than just a powerful mage who drew his magic from the light of the moon. He was more than a man, and he was older than Rafe had believed anyone could ever live to be.

"Not possible," Rafe whispered. "It's simply not possible."

CHAPTER 14

"How is your work coming, my friend?" Errante asked, glancing over Nik's shoulder into the depths of his creation. It was all as much magic to him as the way Nik transferred energy, so he had no idea what he was looking at, which was fine. All mages had secrets, after all.

"It's coming," Nik replied, then grunted as he pulled out a coil of metal, which was eroded in one place to where it was barely holding together. "Found the problem, and I don't think I'll have to build a replacement from scratch. Though if we're here for a week anyway, I'll take the time to check the others and repair them if needed."

"Excellent." Errante peered at the metal. "When you do, let me know, and I shall make certain they are preserved against such wear. I probably should have done it the first time."

Nik shrugged. "I think the magic of the carnival has kept them going for as long as they have, especially since I use them so heavily. You can't save everything, my friend. You worry about the people, and leave the mechanisms to me. I don't mind repairing things that wear out. It helps me understand them better."

"Given that I do not understand them at all, I suppose that makes sense," Errante replied, shaking his head in amusement. "Let me know of anything you may need. Otherwise, I shall leave you to your task."

Satisfied that Nik was proceeding as planned, he next went to visit with the Galliers. Paul had some ideas for new tricks he wanted to add, which would require a change to the way the trapezes were arranged. Since Errante managed the set-ups — though the Galliers were all scrupulous about double checking everything, even if they weren't truly in danger no matter what happened — he needed to know how they wanted things positioned. Paul provided a sketch, which Errante examined, then they went to the Big Top so Errante could move things around. It took a little time to get things perfect, and then he stayed for a few minutes, watching them practice the new stunts, which were even more breathtaking than their old ones. While he kept them safe from harm — which is why they could perform without a net — their abilities were all their own. He'd never seen one of them even come close to a missed catch or do an ill-timed throw.

By the time he was done and left the Galliers to their practice, it was getting close to opening time. He stepped out of the tent, glancing down the Midway for a glimpse of Rafe, who normally spent the last few minutes before the gates admitted their visitors in checking that everyone was in place and ready. Things could and did go wrong from time to time, despite all the magic Errante used to eliminate everything within his power. Things like Nik's capacitor, or a new roustabout needing reassurance that yes, magic was real, or a magical component to a game conflicting with the innate magic of the world they were on. As Ringmaster, Rafe handled the problems that he could, which left Errante free to deal with any larger issues.

But there was no sign of Rafe, no flash of red from his coat, no gleam of gold braid catching the sunlight. Errante frowned, then started down the Midway toward Persephone's tent. He knew Rafe had a special fondness for Persephone, seeing her as something of an aunt, and he visited with her often.

He reached the purple tent and slipped into the dim, cool exterior. He didn't see Persephone, but he found her new assistant, who looked up in surprise from where she was arranging crystals on a side table. Persephone often gave or sold these, depending on the needs of her clients.

"Mr. Ame!"

"Hello, Amelia," he greeted her, giving a slight bow. "Please, call me Errante, as everyone else does." He knew some people stood on ceremony more than others, but he liked to foster as informal a relationship as he could among the core members.

"Errante," she said, smiling. "You know, I studied a couple of different languages in school when I was growing up. And names always fascinated me. I guess yours enchanted me because it was different, but still sort of like mine. But 'Amelia' means 'hardworking' in Hebrew, which I thought was a little boring. Yours, I discovered, was French, and it means 'wandering soul', doesn't it?"

"You are insightful." He inclined his head. A few others over the years had asked about his name, but she was the first in quite some time. "It does."

"If I may ask… were you really given that name as a child? Or is it like your stage name? I mean, given the Carnival and how you… *we*… move around, it's almost scarily appropriate." She was looking at him, hazel eyes wide with genuine interest.

"Errante has been my name for the vast majority of my life," he replied easily, waving a hand. "It is who I think of myself as, my identity, if you will. While it is true I was born to a different name, the meanings are similar. I have not thought of myself as my old name in a very long time." He smiled, gesturing at her neat arrangement of the crystals. "Perhaps you are much like your name as well. Madame tells me you are most diligent in your duties and your lessons."

"I try," she said, flushing in pleasure at the recognition. "I suppose I should get back to it, too, before she returns. Madame stepped out, if you were looking for her."

"Actually, I was in search of Rafe. Have you seen him?"

"He was here earlier," she replied, setting about her task once more. "He walked me back after I returned his coat to him. I had a vision, and it gave me a headache." She looked at him with a shy smile. "He walked me back, since he was worried I might have another vision or something on the way. He's very nice that way. Always looking out for me."

Errante didn't let his expression change, but he could almost see the hearts in her eyes when she spoke of Rafe. She obviously had a crush, and he felt a surge of sympathy for her. Even if Rafe weren't already Errante's lover, he'd never known Rafe to be involved with a woman. It might have missed his notice, but he rather doubted it.

"Rafael is most solicitous, it is true," Errante said quietly. He hoped her regard for Rafe would fade on its own over time, due to lack of reciprocity. He would hate for the nice young woman to have her heart broken because of Rafe having to reject her overtly. "So he left some time ago?"

"Yes, probably an hour ago," she replied. She reached into the box of crystals, pulling out a twisted braid of what seemed to be twigs. She stared at it with a frown. "Oh. I wonder what this is, and what it's doing here."

Errante looked at it as she held it out toward him. He

could sense the magic on it, and he recalled Persephone having shown it to him before, quite some time ago. "I believe that was a bracelet Madame received as a token. If I am remembering correctly, it was from a dryad, and he made it himself from the trees of his sacred grove."

"A *dryad*? An actual tree spirit?" Her eyes were wide and round. "That's so *cool*!"

Errante chuckled. "You will meet many people who are not human while you are with us," he replied. "I am certain Madame has far more unusual tokens somewhere in her collection."

"It makes an interesting piece of jewelry. Kind of boho."

She regarded the bracelet, then smiled and slipped it onto her wrist. Then she suddenly stiffened, eyes growing wide. "Betrayal! Treachery and hatred!"

Alarmed, Errante hurried to her, catching her shoulder to make sure she wouldn't fall. He could see a flicker of magic around her, but it was so brief he almost didn't see it.

"Are you all right?" he asked. "Was it one of your visions?"

Amelia put a hand on her head. "Something like that. An image of fire. And pain, and… I don't know. Treachery? There was a snake in the grass." She shivered, then straightened. "That's two in one day. Not fun."

"You may have been seeing what happened to the Dryad," Errante said, looking her over to make sure she was recovering. He'd stiffened instinctively at the mention of a snake, but she was obviously simply using a turn of phrase, so he forced himself to relax. "Persephone told me that someone set fire to the Dryad's grove. That would indeed be a betrayal, and I imagine it caused him enormous pain."

"I guess?" She shrugged, seeming distressed. "That was some time ago, right? It felt so… recent? Or like it hasn't happened yet? It's more jumbled than other visions I've had."

"No doubt because of the Carnival. Time is… fluid here."

He explained, hoping to ease her mind. "Even though the event already happened, from the perspective of the Carnival, it could lie along a more future timeline for you. Nik once called it temporal dissonance, when the energy of an event occurs along different Paths for various people."

She seemed to accept that explanation. Then she shuddered. "I suppose I'll have to get used to the feeling."

Since she seemed to have recovered, he released her and stepped back. "Perhaps you should go lie down? Magic can be very exhausting sometimes. Madame will understand. I'll find her and tell her."

"Thank you, Mr. A… I mean, Errante," she said, smiling weakly. "I do feel drained."

He nodded, shooing her toward the back curtain. "Everything will be fine. You rest."

She nodded, then disappeared behind the curtain. Errante shook his head. Having two mages just coming into their powers was going to keep him and Persephone busy, he could tell.

Fortunately, he met up with Persephone as he stepped outside the tent.

"Your young charge had another Vision, and it seems to have disturbed her a bit," he explained.

"Par for the course," she replied, waving a hand at him. Then she gave him a shrewd look. "We need to talk, but later. Men. Idiots. But I repeat myself."

With that cryptic statement, she entered the tent. He turned away, puzzled over her words, then shrugged. No doubt someone had annoyed her, but he could deal with it later.

There was still no sign of Rafe. He gave a quick glance toward the arch where crowds were already gathering, eager to experience the delights and distractions within. As one of the more experienced roustabouts hurried by, he stopped him.

"Simeon, please see that the gates open on time, even if Rafe and I are not here. It seems something may have come up that requires my attention."

"Right-O, Mr. Ame," Simeon replied with a grin. "I'll see to it, never fear."

"Thank you." With that, he put the operation of the Carnival into what was the equivalent of automatic pilot, and then he went to look for Rafe.

Several minutes of searching didn't reveal Rafe in any of his usual haunts, so he turned toward Rafe's quarters. Perhaps he'd simply overslept, exhausted after their exertions of the night and morning. The thought made Errante smile, but then it faded, as he recalled Amelia had claimed Rafe had walked her back to the tent after she'd returned his coat and hat. So Rafe *had* been awake. But where was he now?

Alarmed, he quickened his pace, reaching the Rafe's 'trailer', which was set away from the others. He tried the door, finding it unlocked; not that there was any lock in the Carnival that would not have yielded to his will.

He stepped into the dim living area, but a quick glance showed it was empty. So he moved to the bedroom, cracking the door open and peering inside. His knees went weak with relief as he saw Rafe sitting on the bed, looking down at a book in his hands.

"Rafael? Are you all right?" he asked, moving into the room.

Slowly Rafe looked up from the book, and the torment and fear in his gaze ripped at Errante's heart.

"I don't know," he said, his voice ragged.

"What happened?" Errante stepped closer, holding up a hand, intending to lay it on Rafe's shoulder to comfort him.

But then his heart seemed to stop, as Rafe moved *away* from him, looking at Errante as though he'd never seen him before.

"I was reading," he said dully. "Tell me, Khonsu, am I just a toy to you? Or did you think I would never discover the truth?"

CHAPTER 15

Rafe watched as Errante froze in place. Even though his body was immobile, an expression of such profound pain and grief twisted his face that it cut through Rafe's sense of anger and betrayal like a knife. He wasn't certain what he'd expected when he confronted Errante with the truth. He hadn't thought ahead that far, too overwhelmed by his own feelings to even consider Errante's. But now, seeing an ancient anguish he'd ever expected, he wanted to rush to his lover, embrace him, and tell him everything was going to be fine. And yet he couldn't, because he didn't know that it *would* be fine after all. How did someone wrap their mind around the thought of their lover being a deity? How did they live with the knowledge once they'd accepted it? So he did nothing, their gazes locked for a time that could have been minutes or hours.

Finally, Errante drew a breath. "I have not heard that name in a long time," he said. The pain was still in his eyes, as though a cloud had obscured the starlight Rafe usually saw in them.

"But it is you, isn't it?" Rafe asked. He held up the book so

Errante could read the title embossed in gilt letters on its front. "I had completely forgotten about the book I bought in the world where… where I found my powers," he said, stumbling over the mention of the incident even now. "Amelia had a vision and reminded me of it." He drew in a breath, trying to steady his racing pulse. "I knew you were powerful. I knew I probably couldn't comprehend how powerful, but I thought you were a man like me. A mortal. Not a *god*!"

Errante remained unmoving, his features stoic. It was an expression Rafe hadn't seen on Errante's face since he'd been a child. "And what is a god to you, Rafael?" he asked softly. There was no anger in his voice, no accusation, but no defensiveness, either. "Is it an omniscient, all-knowing being that inhabits some paradise and revels in the adulation and sacrifices of their followers? A creature who lives for worship and adoration, and throws petty tantrums when they aren't received? Or perhaps a being so vast and powerful that they are unknowable, unreachable, and so perfect they cannot be imagined? For I assure you, I am none of these. I *am* a man. I have powers, and believe me, those powers have brought me more pain, more uncertainty and fear than you can imagine. I have cursed them in the past, and wished to be rid of them, but too many people suffered for me to have them, and so I endure. But for all that, I am a man with a soul. I can love, and I can bleed. I was born. And someday I will die."

Rafe simply looked at him, thoughts racing. He had so many questions, so many fears. "This book says you were a god, born of gods. Mut and Amun. Is that true?"

"My parents were Mut and Amun, yes," Errante replied. That expression of grief crossed his face again, and for a moment he looked *old*. Not that he aged, but a sadness and pain seemed to weigh him down, wiping the life from his face the way years often did to those who were weary of living. "They were powerful mages, who did everything they could to help those around them, but they were not gods — or if so, only in the ways of people who didn't have a true understanding of how magic worked, of what it could and could not do. And they are dead now, nothing but dust and memory, betrayed by someone they once loved who wanted their power for his own."

"I… I just can't understand," Rafe said. Again, he wanted to run to Errante, to erase the pain he knew he was causing, but he held himself still. He needed to know, and he felt, on some level, that Errante needed to tell him. "Please, tell me the truth. All of it."

"I would never lie to you, but I never wished to burden you, or anyone else, with details that can neither be fully explained, nor understood." Errante's voice was deep and full of sadness. "I grew up in Egypt, a land of vast wealth and power. Magic was my heritage. It is common for powerful mages to produce other powerful mages, so my abilities were my birthright, one I had because of my parents. My family was prominent indeed, and my playmates were the sons of pharaohs and viziers. It was common for people of power to consider themselves akin to deities. The pharaoh actually *was* considered a god and exercised power almost beyond imagining. But my parents taught me humility and care for all. I was told that at my death my soul would be weighed and judged, as were the souls of all men. That my value was no more or less than the lowliest laborer or highest king. It was what I had done with my life that would determine my place in the hereafter."

"And you believed that?" Rafe asked. What he'd read of the Egyptian death beliefs seemed very complex. Errante had never struck him as being religious.

"I still do." Errante shrugged slightly. "I am no more and no less than you, no matter what you think I should believe or what you believe yourself. Older, yes, perhaps, if age confers anything other than the knowledge you still will die. Religion is a social construct designed to explain the world in terms that can be understood. What I will tell you is that one truth I have discovered in my long, long years is that every creature, every being, every person with a soul longs to understand the world in which they exist. In civilizations where science has not explained the world's mysteries to its inhabitants, they make up tales to fill the void of their knowledge. I know you studied much with Calliope, read the tales of heroes and villains from a thousand worlds. All those stories are the attempts of people to understand and explain. If I did not know of how storms worked, it might be comforting to think of a Thor throwing bolts of lightning, or of a Boreas sending the icy winds of the north down to chill the earth. When in fact Thor was a mage who had power with electricity, and Boreas another who could summon wind."

"So the gods existed?" Rafe asked, desperately wanting to understand, to believe that somehow he fit in with Errante, that he could be enough to someone so powerful. "But as mages?"

"They were certainly not divine beings. Some held their worlds as their playthings, drunk with power, but they were mortal all the same. To put it in a way that might be more relatable — to a man who has nothing, another man who has a home, no matter how humble, might seem to be a king. A man who owned a country might seem like a god, even though he was still just a man." Errante paused, watching Rafe intently. "Would it pain you to know your adoptive mother, who loved you, nurtured you, and gave you the strength to be the man you are, is, by the people of her native land, considered a goddess, daughter of a god? One of nine sisters who served as the inspiration for all the great art ever created in that land?"

"My… mother?" That information made Rafe's head spin. "You mean she really *is* Calliope, the muse?"

"She is the Calliope of whom that is believed, yes. The muse of epic poetry — which she taught to you, and her tattoos reflected. But does that make her any less the mother who nurtured and cared for you?"

"I— I—" Rafe stumbled over the words as he tried to imagine the mother he knew and loved as existing on Olympus, her father Zeus looking at her with approval. But his heart told him what his head was still trying to accept: she was his mother. She loved him and always had. That made it more real to him, somehow, though he still had a hard time wrapping his mind fully around it. "She is my mother," he replied. "Then who else? Persephone? Is she really *that* Persephone?"

"No, she simply liked that name more than her own, and she would have told you all this herself, if you had ever asked," Errante replied. "She is Skuld, a Norn, one known as one aspect of fate in old Norse mythology, and she was once a Valkyrie. She told me they did not choose the slain, merely carried the valiant dead from the battlefield. She lived through the end of her own civilization, saw it collapse and be consumed as the supposed 'gods' of her culture fought each other to the end. Again, the acts of men, not gods."

"Ragnarok?" Rafe scrubbed his face with his hands. Persephone didn't just read Fate, she *was* Fate?

"Indeed. You read books, Rafael. What some consider myths and legends were once history to others. And as stories do, they change in the telling. Men become heroes, heroes become legends, and legends become gods. But when you take a step back and see them for what they are and observe them within their own lifetimes and not with the distance and romance imparted by history, you see they are souls traveling their Path through the universe. Some are forever tied to the place of their origin, and their stories become lost. Others Travel more widely and are remembered. Often their tales become changed, enhanced, or exaggerated in the telling. But in the end, they are simply people. Flawed, noble, weak, powerful, heroic, or villainous according to their nature and their choices. Nothing more. As I am no more than you, nor than anyone else in this Carnival, be it Persephone, or Nik, or one of the roustabouts. Every soul matters. Every soul is judged the same in the end by what they did in life to help others. Every soul has a tale to tell, no matter how long or brief their life is."

Rafe didn't know what to say, as Errante continued to look at him. There was such a stillness to him, a sense of distance, that it brought to mind the phrase 'remote as the moon'. It fit him in that moment, and Rafe felt his confusion returning. Along with the question he needed to know the answer to. It burned within him, leaving him afraid.

"What am I to you?" he asked. "I'm not a god. I'm not even powerful. I'm just… me."

"You are Rafael," Errante said. A light shone through the clouds darkening his eyes, dim but present, and there was a crack in his detachment. "You are the Sun. You give light to my darkness. I have spent five thousand years walking my Path, and in all that time, on all those worlds beyond count, I have never found love. Until you. You are my universe. And, without you, I do not wish to continue." He paused. "But you may go, if you desire, and I will take you wherever you wish to be, and you can live the life of your choosing, with all the riches it is within my power to give you. Live freely doing as you will, without ever having to worry that I would be like Zeus and take vengeance because you cannot return my feelings because of what I am. I have never wanted worship, not from you or anyone else. I would give up my magic for you, take the Carnival to some place of your choosing and live out my life with you in the span of years a normal man might expect, if that is your wish. What does that make me in your eyes, Rafael? Is it a flaw or a strength that the only thing I desire in all the times of all the worlds is your love?"

Rafe felt tears sting his eyes. He'd been so hung up on the fact that Errante was so much *more* than he'd ever imagined was possible. It had made him feel small, somehow as powerless as a child when faced with the knowledge of their own limits, that they can't jump high enough to reach the sky no matter how hard they tried. He'd wanted to place that sense of futility at Errante's feet, instead of on his own head where it belonged. Rafe had taken counsel of his own fears and insecurities, but Errante had faced them with strength and dignity. And despite everything, despite all his power, all he was and all he had and all that he could do, Errante asked for one thing. How could Rafe deny him that, especially when it was what he wanted in return?

He remembered his own words to Amelia, an hour or a lifetime ago. That Errante valued people, valued their choices and always respected that they had a right to whatever choice they made. If Errante was with him, it was because he chose to be. And no matter what Rafe chose, Errante would honor his words. Rafe had nothing to fear except the chaos within himself.

"Is it?" he asked.

"It is." Errante said the words, so simple, yet so full of love and tenderness, that Rafe dropped the book, hurling himself from the bed and into Errante's arms. He was held so tightly that he could hardly breathe, but he clung to Errante just as fiercely.

"I'm sorry I doubted," he murmured against Errante's neck. "It was just more than I could process, and I was afraid. But you're all I want, too. You never have to give up the

Carnival for me, not ever. I love it, and I love you, and I never want to be anywhere but by your side."

He felt Errante tremble against him, and he pulled back, seeing the tears in Errante's eyes. He'd never, in all the years he'd know him, ever seen Errante cry. To know that he had been the one to cause so much pain tore at his heart.

"No, please, don't cry," Rafe begged. "I'm sorry, so sorry for—"

Errante lifted a hand, placing it against Rafe's lips. "They are tears of happiness and relief," he said. "I thought I was about to lose you. I have never cried over loss. I have been through it many times, and I have learned to face it with clear eyes. But joy is a stranger I have no defenses against. All I would ask in the future is that you come to me, and ask me what you need to know. I will tell you."

"I didn't know what was in the book," Rafe admitted. "Amelia said in her Vision that I needed to heed its words or I would lose everything I love. I wasn't expecting what I found."

"In that case, we will go through it together, and we shall see what lessons it provides," Errante said. "Later. Right now, I want to hold you and be held in return. The Carnival can go on without us."

Rafe nodded, then his lips were captured in a kiss that was as close to perfect as he'd ever imagined a kiss could be. He gave himself over to it, wanting Errante more than anything else in the universe, and feeling just as wanted in return.

Errante was right — whatever the book had to say, they could discover it later. Right now, he preferred to teach Errante Ame just how much Rafael Harper loved him. And if he were to tempt Fate and court destruction in daring to love a god, then so be it. That would be the tale *his* soul would happily tell.

CHAPTER 16

The afternoon was well advanced by the time they had finally risen from the bed and gotten dressed once more. Errante had sent a message to Nik to act as his backup, to reassure everyone that nothing was wrong, and that Errante's and Rafe's attention was simply required elsewhere to deal with something that had come up. It wasn't the first time something like it had occurred, so they had had the time, uninterrupted, to strengthen their bond. And, after Rafe mentioned they'd been overheard, for Errante to make certain that Rafe's quarters were as completely soundproofed as Persephone's.

He didn't mind that his closest friend knew; Persephone would tell no one, though she would probably tease and torment both of them mercilessly. But it wouldn't do for there to be speculation among the rest of their friends. Not that he didn't trust them, but even a casual conversation being overheard by an outsider might be enough to put Rafe in danger. He knew Rafe considered him paranoid, but Errante had stayed hidden for five millennia only by magic and discretion. He wasn't willing to drop his guard yet.

Once dressed, they moved into Rafe's living area, and Rafe brought the book. They settled onto the sofa, and Errante spread it open between them, reading swiftly over the introduction.

"Karnak is in Thebes, the area where my family had their power," he explained to Rafe. "Not the Thebes of the Greeks, but the one in Egypt, along the Nile." He pointed to a picture of a temple complex, feeling a surge of homesickness he hadn't felt in longer than he could remember. It was in ruins, but enough remained that he could easily identify it. "I cannot believe it is still standing. That was my home, where I grew up."

"Really?" Rafe peered at the structure, which still held much of its beauty and grace. "Wow. So your family were the rulers?"

"Not exactly." Errante considered. "The Pharaohs were the rulers; we were magicians and nobles. We had both magical and temporal powers, and my parents were much beloved by the people. Especially my mother." He smiled sadly. "She was the most incredible woman, Rafe. I can see why, after her death, people would revere her as a goddess."

Rafe smiled and put a hand over Errante's, giving it a comforting squeeze. "Why do I get the feeling you take after her?"

"If I do, then it would be my honor," he replied, but he leaned over to give Rafe a brief kiss. "Now, let us continue to look for what we must learn."

He flipped the page, which showed more of the complex, and he frowned. "I see they combined my father with Ra. This is what I meant by things getting confused over time, when the stories become jumbled. There was Ra, and there was my father, Amun. They were allies, true, especially when things grew bad with S… our enemy." Even now he found it hard to say the name, so he hurried on. "Ra was much older than my father. They were distant cousins, but Ra is the most powerful mage from my country, possibly in the world. Ra was centuries old by the time I was born, and it was he who guided the Pharaohs."

"He drew his magic from the sun as well?" Rafe's fingers skimmed over a picture which showed an engraving of a hawk-headed man with a disk on his head. Lines of light from an overhead sun were depicted as radiating toward him.

"He did," Errante acknowledged. "Many mages drew power from the light of the sun — do not forget that all life on a world receives its energy, either directly or indirectly, from the sun."

"Ah." Rafe nodded. "That makes sense. So let me guess: he had a bigger magical reservoir than anyone, and that's why he was so powerful."

"In part. He was also wise." Errante turned another page. This time he flushed, feeling embarrassed as he saw his own name heading a section. He read it over swiftly. "Well, they seem to have gotten several things right, but I find the thought of having been worshipped... uncomfortable. Especially..." He trailed off and looked away.

"What? What is it?" Rafe asked, his fingers once again covering Errante's, concern evident in his furrowed brow. "Is it that you don't feel worthy of so much respect?"

"Something like that." Drawing in a breath, Errante pointed out a section labeled *Set*. "I will not speak his name, but you can read it there easily enough. That is my enemy. He is responsible for the death of my family, of my friends."

Rafe traced the word with his finger, then a shudder ran down his spine. "That's why there are no snakes in the carnival, not even stuffed ones or rubber ones as prizes?"

Errante nodded. "I fear him gaining entrance somehow through that mechanism."

"So what happened?" Rafe asked softly.

With a shudder of his own, Errante turned his hand over beneath Rafe's and clasped it tightly. "It is easier to show you. Do not be frightened."

With that, he pulled Rafe into his memories.

AROUND THEM, the desert stretched unbroken, sand dunes undulating toward the horizon in all directions. "This is your spirit body, your *ka*," he explained to Rafael, pointing to their transparent forms. "Nothing can see or hurt you, because this is just a memory, and not even one of mine, but of my mother's. I was a child, not even eighteen years old. I believe that is why the book depicts me as a child."

The sky overhead was dark with clouds that flashed lightning, an odd sight to see over a land so barren. But in the distance, coming closer, was a pounding that was not thunder. They flew across the sands toward the sound and quickly found its source.

A battle. A horrific, violent, bloody battle, pitting man against man in a combat to the death.

Two armies faced off in the wastes, the curved blades of khopesh and the wickedly sharp edges of battle axes clanging against shields. Often they cut through and into the soft bodies beneath. Blood, brains, and entrails spilled on the sands, red, then turning black beneath the sandaled feet of the soldiers. As one body fell, it disappeared, and another rose to take its place. Even more horrifying than the massacre was the absolute silence from the combatants. There were no grunts, no cries of anguish, no shouts of victory when a blow struck home. There was nothing on their faces but grim determination, as if each man there battled not just for his life, but for his soul. The armies surged together, neither gaining nor losing ground.

"This is not my world but a sort of demi-plane, where magicians of great power come to counsel, or to practice… or to battle."

"Are they real people?" Rafe asked, his horror evident in his tone.

"They were. Armies of the dead, caught up in a war not of their making or their choosing." Errante pointed up to the sky, where several more people floated. These were different, though, dressed in robes of pure white. Flashes of energy splashed between them.

Errante raised their *ka* up into the air, where it became apparent that there were two men fighting against many. One had the body of a man, but the head of something more like a dog, though it was no dog that had ever existed in reality. A snake was twined about his waist, and he snarled as he fended off the magical attacks from the people who faced him: a man with a falcon's head, a woman whose crown looked like antlers, another woman with the head of a black cat. The ally of the dog-headed man had a snake head, but he was obviously not as powerful as the dog-headed mage.

"My great enemy," he explained to Rafe, pointing to Set. "He is allied here to Apep, though in the future he will simply absorb Apep's power for his own. As he absorbed the power of his brother, Osiris, and then murdered him." He indicated the other group. "Horus the Younger, son of Osiris. Isis, his mother, and Isis's and Osiris's sister, Bast. These are the children of Ra, locked in a battle for dominance and power."

Another figure emerged from behind where Rafe and Errante hovered, her enormous, black wings sweeping the sky. She did not fight; instead, she touched Isis, Horus, and Bast, and they grew stronger, fighting back against Set with more energy.

"My mother, Mut," he whispered, unable to take his eyes from the sight of her. "Her powers were over life, but she allied herself to Isis and her allies in trying to defeat our enemy — as did my father, Amun. But for every one of them that fell in battle, our enemy became more powerful."

Mut winged higher, and abruptly Set targeted her with a blast that sent her plunging toward the ground. Abruptly, the memory ended.

Rafe drew in a shaky breath as they were once again in his quarters. "That was horrifying."

"It was a war that went on... well, I doubt time had much relevance in that place."

"So... your enemy won?" Rafe asked softly.

"Yes, and no." Errante gave a twisted smile. "He wanted the power of all the mages, even his father, Ra. But no one could approach Ra against his will — he was that powerful. And much power was wasted in battles such as you just witnessed. Raising armies of the dead to fight is an intensive use of magic, even on a demi-plane. But whatever was left of every mage that fell in battle, Set took, using their magic to enhance his own, making it harder to fight him."

"How could he stand against so many?" Rafe tapped the book. "There were dozens of you, weren't there? And if half the things I saw in here are true, perhaps hundreds of lesser power? How could he defeat them all?"

Errante sighed sadly. "He had absorbed many of the minor ones before he ever went after his brother. You have to understand, Egypt was enormous, and there were hundreds of minor mages across the land. Mages tended toward solitude, so my enemy spent decades, maybe even centuries, taking their power. The first sign that things were bad was when he murdered Osiris. It sparked the war between the factions, but by the time it started, my enemy — *our* enemy — was nearly invincible."

"Why didn't Ra do something?" There was outrage in Rafe's expression. "Didn't he have enough power to stop his own son?"

Errante ran a hand through his hair. "I have asked myself that many, many times. Remember, Ra was incredibly old. He may even have been the first mage, and perhaps he really was a god, I do not know, for I never met him. He may have feared that if his son obtained *his* powers, he would be unstoppable. I do not know what my enemy wants with so much power."

"But you escaped," Rafe said. "I'm so glad you did. Is that why you think he pursues you? He wants your power?"

Errante winced. He sometimes hated the fact that he could flee when others couldn't, but he drew in a deep breath. "In part. But there is more you should know, Rafael. I have power, but it is not what I was born with. My mother... she could easily transfer magic, as you saw in that memory. She was a vessel of magical energy, and she used it to recharge other mages. I believe our enemy feared and yet coveted her more than any of the others. With her, he really could take on his father."

"But isn't she dead?" Rafe asked, frowning in confusion. "He didn't get her power?"

"Yes, she is dead," Errante acknowledged. "But... he never got her power, nor the power she was given by my father, my stepmother, and my aunts and uncles." He drew in a deep breath, seeing the question in Rafe's eyes, and knowing he needed to speak the words, even as he saw the dawning of understanding in Rafe's expression. "He never got it... because *I* did."

For a moment Rafe just stared at him, then he blew out a breath. "I suppose it's a good thing I love you, because that's honestly a little frightening, you know."

Errante sighed, squeezing Rafe's hand. "I know. You see

why I hesitated to tell you any of this? It is a great deal to take in. Even I find it overwhelming, and I lived through it."

Rafe nodded. "I can imagine. So… that's why you can transfer power to me? Because of what your mother gave you?"

"Yes." Errante smiled, but he knew it was a sad expression. "From her, the power to give energy. From my father, a certain dominion over weather, which is why the Carnival stays fair no matter the weather of where we are located. My aunt Sekhmet gave me the strength to fight and the power to heal. Sekhmet's husband, Ptah, gave me the ability to understand all languages. My other aunt, Ma'at, gave me my sense of justice and the desire for all creatures to be treated fairly. And from my stepmother, I received the power to stay hidden in the shadows if I desire. None of them, save my mother, imparted all their power to me — remember, they were still fighting our enemy when I left. But they each gave me part of their gifts. I have tried to use them wisely, to act as they would have me act, and use them to keep my power safe from the one who caused their deaths."

"You know they are dead for certain?" Rafe leaned closer, offering the comfort of his presence.

"I… felt it." Errante shivered. "Through the link of their power to me, I felt their passing, and… like some residual trickle of power, as though in their last moments they sent what remained so that our enemy could not get it. But my mother…"

"You saw her die." Something flared in Rafe's eyes, and a brief expression of confusion crossed his face. "Sorry, I thought I remembered something for a moment, but now it's gone."

Errante watched for a moment, but whatever had crossed Rafe's mind seemed to have been brief. "Yes, I saw her die. She was holding my hand as she gave me all her power. Until that moment, I could Travel, yes, but it was a limited ability, only on my world, and mostly just to places I already knew. I could also see the Paths of others, but again, it was not something of great utility, though I helped where I could to guide them on their way. It was not until my mother gave me her powers and told me to guide a young woman along her Path, that I learned how far I could truly Travel."

Rafe stared at him. "So even your first act with all that power was to help someone else? Do you realize how unusual that is?" he asked, but when Errante only shrugged, embarrassed by the admiration in his tone, he asked another question. "What happened next?"

"It was, well, difficult," he admitted. "I helped her to her destination, surprised to find us in a world like and yet unlike our own. There were people in a setting that was strange but not frightening. Where Egypt had deserts, with tents and buildings of stone, the people we were among lived in lush forests with buildings of wood. Yet they were as golden skinned as we, with black hair, so we did not stand out as being remarkable. With Ptah's gift, I could understand them, and I learned I could transfer that gift to my companion. We claimed to be travelers from a far land, and they welcomed us. I stayed for a short time, to see her marriage to a man in our new community. But I knew I was still in danger, so I left, not wishing to bring any harm to Neith or to my..." He stopped, frowning. "What is wrong?"

Rafe had gone rigid, eyes wide. "Neith? Her name was Neith? I... do you... can you remember the man she married?"

Errante frowned. It was his turn to be confused. "I am not sure. I think... Sachem? He was a chief..."

Rafe shot to his feet, spilling the book on the floor. "I remember! I remember that!" he said, staring at Errante with wide eyes.

"How?" he asked, blinking in astonishment at the way Rafe was pacing in agitation. "Did my memories somehow leak over?"

"No! Don't you see?" Rafe shook his head, then drew in a deep breath. "I never remembered until you said their names. Errante, impossible as it sounds... Neith and Sachem were my parents."

CHAPTER 17

Errante was gaping at him. Rafe didn't think he'd ever seen such a surprised expression on Errante's face, not even when he'd spoken Errante's true name. Had it been only that morning? It didn't seem possible, but apparently it was a day for revelations.

His time before the Carnival had always been a mystery, not just to him, but even to Persephone and Calliope. All he had been told was that he was the lone survivor of a village that had been devastated, though no one had ever disclosed the circumstances, and he had never asked. Perhaps he'd never grown curious because, deep down, he already knew what happened.

"How is it possible?" Errante asked, still lost. "When the Carnival came to that village, I had no memory of myself having been there before. I should have…"

"Five thousand years is a long time," Rafe said absently. He was trying to recall what had happened, but while he could now remember the names of his parents, and their faces, everything else was still hazy, like seeing through a dense fog. There were flashes of things, like a wooden chair, a dirt floor, the scent of pine boughs, the rustle of wind in the trees, but nothing concrete, other than his parents. After so many years of having a big nothing where those memories had been, it was almost too much to wrap his mind around, and yet he wanted more.

"I suppose." Errante rose to his feet, then took Rafe by the shoulders, urging him down onto the sofa. "Sit. You have had even more to take in than I had thought possible."

"It's so close," Rafe whispered. "So close. I never wanted to know before, but now… Now I think I *need* to know."

"What do you need to know?" Errante asked, holding both Rafe's hands in his.

"Who they were. My parents," Rafe replied slowly. He smiled crookedly. "You and I are, at least through my mother, from the same world. The ruins in that book. Some of them might have been her home, too. Do you remember her from before you left? Who she was, who her parents were?"

An expression of sadness crossed Errante's face. "I am sorry to say that I do not. I believe she may have been a handmaiden to my mother, but I cannot be certain. Many people came and went in our home, and remember I was a boy, preoccupied with my own thoughts and desires — and I had known from a very early age that women did not attract me. Once we Traveled, we both remained silent about our lives before. It was safer not to speak of it, even in our own language. She was grateful I had brought her to a place where she found love and acceptance, and I was grateful that her Path set me upon my own. Other than that, as I told you, I stayed only a short time. Neith would not be in danger from my enemy, not unless I was there as well, so I left."

Rafe nodded. "I understand. But you saved her, and I'm grateful for that." He snorted. "Not only did you save my life as a child, if it weren't for you, I wouldn't even exist."

"Then I am more grateful than ever to your mother. She

not only gave me a purpose when I desperately needed one, she gave me you."

"I wish I could remember more about her," Rafe said. Then he sighed. Perhaps Errante was right, and it would come to him. Given it was Errante's words that had spurred his memory anyway, perhaps hearing the rest would spark something more. "So what did you do then?"

"I Traveled that world for a while, and in a land far from where I left Neith, I got the idea for the Carnival. Not as it exists now, of course. It has grown. Then I left that world, following a Path that called to me. I helped someone who was lost, and then I found Persephone. I told her of my plans, and she accompanied me on my Travels. Slowly, my little band grew. It took a long time to become what it is now, and everywhere I went, I poured magic into the Carnival. Many people have come and gone, but a few have remained from the beginning." Errante squeezed Rafe's hands gently. "I wish I could tell you more about your mother's family, but I never knew. I will say she was kind and loving. Her husband fell in love with her, and she with him almost from the moment we arrived in that village. He was the chieftain there, a strong and capable man. The land we were in had no central government. It was a collection of villages and small towns that remained in contact mostly through river traffic. Each village worked hard to fill its own needs through hunting, fishing, and farming, trading for things from other villages when they had excess. It was a simple way of life, but your mother said it was perfect for her, so I left her to her happiness."

"I'm sorry her happiness turned out to be so brief," Rafe replied. The burning need to *know* his parents was tempered by Errante's words, but he could still feel it within him. He bit his lip, and then he decided to ask the question hovering in the air between them. "Would you take me there?"

Errante closed his eyes as though the request pained him, but then he opened them again. "I will, if that is your wish," he said. "I cannot, unfortunately, take you back to when your parents were still alive." He held up a hand, forestalling the question that sprang instantly to Rafe's lips. "And before you ask, no, I do not know why. I just know what *is*. I could never overlap myself in a world, and since I was still on that world for some time after I left Neith, I cannot go back there during that time. I suspect the point when the Carnival returned and you were found was not long after my first departure from there — perhaps three years linearly, and yet nearly five thousand later for me. Nik asked me about it once, and when I explained, he said it was undoubtedly to avoid a paradox."

"I still want to go back," Rafe said. "Please."

"Very well." Errante nodded, though he didn't look happy. "Before we go, however, we need to finish our tasks here, which will take a day or two more. And in the meantime, you must talk with Persephone."

"Persephone?" Rafe was surprised. "I know she can't read my future, so why…"

"Because she was *there*," Errante said. "I did not see what happened, and when we go, I am going to insist that she and Nik accompany you, as I cannot. But before I set foot on that world again, you are going to have to accept something. And I mean truly accept it, know it in your heart as surely as you know your own name and your magic. Otherwise, I will refuse to take you there."

Rafe couldn't imagine why Errante seemed to be so resistant. "What must I accept?"

"That nothing that occurred there was your fault."

ERRANTE HAD REFUSED to answer any more questions, while Rafe bit back his impatience and followed his lover toward the purple tent. Errante moved with single-minded purpose, a man on a mission, ignoring even those of the carnival who called out greetings to him. When they finally reached the purple tent, Errante paused outside since the flap was closed. It was only a few moments, however, before someone came out, startled to see Errante standing so close, tapping his foot with impatience. As soon as the man departed, Errante held back the flap and gestured for Rafe to enter.

He stepped inside, and Persephone rose from her table, her expression full of concern. When Errante entered right after him, she braced her hands on her hips. "Now what? I swear lately with you two, it's always something!"

Rafe shook his head. "Ask *him*," he said, jerking a thumb at Errante. "One moment I'm asking him if he can take me to see where I was born, and the next moment he's insisting that I have to talk to you and it's not my fault. But he won't say *what* isn't my fault. He just took off for here like he was being chased by demons or something."

"Your assistant?" Errante asked, his voice calm as though he hadn't just practically sprinted through the Carnival.

"Still in the back, lying down," Persephone said. "Whatever the two of you have put the poor girl through lately has been a bit much for her. But yes, Errante was right to bring you to me. He didn't see what happened there, but I did."

"What happened?" Rafe asked, throwing up his hands. "Calliope said my village was destroyed. She said something about brigands having killed everyone." He felt frustration rising, no doubt because there were simply too many mysteries for him, even though he'd grown up in an entire Carnival of them. These were personal, and that made it different.

"Yes, there were brigands," Persephone said. She came

around to stand in front of Rafe, meeting his gaze levelly. "Everyone in the village was dead, and we could see where people had been slaughtered. Then there was your home, where we found you. You were sitting in the middle of a room, and the people whom I assume were your parents were nearby. In fact, your mother was curled around you as though trying to protect you. I won't go into detail, but their deaths were by the sword and weren't easy. Of the brigands, there was no sign at all."

It was difficult to hear her speak so offhandedly of violent death, especially when it came to his parents. But Rafe nodded curtly. "That's more than I knew before, but really, I hadn't wanted to know. So I was a little kid, right? Not much more than a baby? So how is any of that my fault?"

"None of it is your fault!" Both Errante and Persephone spoke up at the same time. He felt Errante's hand on his shoulder, but Persephone waved Errante to silence.

"Let me handle this." She looked at Rafe again. "One thing for which we had no explanation was the other damage to the house, the surrounding area, and the entire village."

"Other damage?" Rafe asked, frowning. Then it hit him. "*Fire* damage?"

"Yes." Persephone said simply. "Errante wasn't there. He didn't see it, but I did. Damage radiated out from where you sat, as if you were the epicenter of a powerful blast. The timbers were still warm. I couldn't see your Fate, but I thought perhaps your mother had some magical ability, and as she was dying, she unleashed it to protect you. That might be the case, Rafe, and it is what I thought for years. I doubt we will ever know, short of locating a ghost in the area, if there are any. Yes, you manifested a small ability with fire, but nothing strong enough to do the amount of damage we saw in that village."

Rafe's heart was pounding, and he felt lightheaded. "But now… you think *I* did it?"

"Perhaps. Perhaps not." Persephone shrugged. "But what you should take away from this, and what Errante feared you might not believe, is that they were all dead before whatever happened. Perhaps the brigands were incinerated in the blast, which would be odd because your parents' bodies weren't. If your mother did it to protect you, I would expect that to be the case. Perhaps you let off that blast because you needed help and didn't know what else to do. Or maybe when your life and your mother's life were threatened, you reacted out of survival instinct. But believe me, there is one thing I know for certain." She reached up, putting her hands on either side of his head, and looked deeply into his eyes. "No innocents were harmed by what you did. If you killed anyone, it was only evil people who had sealed their own Fates the moment they started murdering your village and your family. You must believe that. By the souls of myself and my sisters, I believe it to be the truth."

He looked into the depths of Persephone's eyes and saw the truth in them. She fully believed every word she had spoken; he could not doubt that. He wanted to believe her, wanted to believe he wasn't, even as a child, the kind of person who could wantonly destroy. And while he could accept her words and their logic, something deep inside him quivered in fear, as it had when he'd first unleashed his magic when he'd been stabbed.

"All right, I accept that," he said, keeping his voice even. "It's logical, and if I had done it in fear or even anger, I wouldn't be held responsible because of my age." He shivered, feeling Errante's hand tighten on his shoulder. It braced him, and he could almost feel the love and concern Errante was radiating.

Persephone was still cradling his face, looking at him,

perhaps reading him with whatever abilities she had, despite her claim of not being able to see his Fate. "See that you accept it," she said, then patted his cheeks gently before stepping back. "You're a good man, Rafe. We just wanted to be sure *you* knew that before you faced your past."

"So, I accept it," he said, then turned his head to look over his shoulder at Errante. "Does that mean you can take me back now?"

Errante gave him a searching glance of his own. "I will," he said. "Not without reservations, and as far as you stepping out of the Carnival, I am not happy about it. But if it is still your desire, we will go."

"It is." Rafe sighed, then scrubbed at his face with both hands. "There is something I need to find there. I know it. Something important. But I can't remember what it is."

"Give it time, Rafe," Persephone advised. "And get some rest." She looked at Errante sharply. "And by rest, I mean *sleep*, not more of—"

She cut off abruptly, turning toward the rear of the tent, just as Amelia pushed aside the diaphanous draperies and stepped out. The poor girl looked pale and wan, but she smiled at Rafe and Errante.

"Sorry, I didn't know anyone was out here," she said. "I'll just go back..."

"It's fine, dear, we were done," Persephone said. "The rest doesn't seem to have helped much, does it?"

"I feel so drained," she admitted. "Maybe I'm coming down with something."

"We'll go see Peter. I'm sure one of his potions will help," Persephone said soothingly. She looked at Errante and Rafe sternly. "Rest. Both of you. I suspect we have an even busier time ahead."

Once she herded Amelia out of the tent, Rafe turned to Errante.

"Do you think she *saw* that, or I am reading too much into things?"

Errante shrugged. "I could not tell, but I am not about to tempt Fate. Come, you. Time for sleep. We have a few days before Nik will finish up his work. But then, yes, we will return to your home world and see what there is to see."

With that, he guided them back out into the fading light of the day, and they headed toward Rafe's quarters. There was too much to take in, and he was suddenly feeling over-whelmed and exhausted. For once, all he wanted to do in bed with Errante was to sleep and not dream.

CHAPTER 18

The days had seemed to crawl by, and Rafe was practically vibrating by the time the Carnival closed on their last day. Nik had hurried to finish his capacitor once he'd been told that they needed to move as soon as possible, and Rafe had the feeling Errante might have ignored a few other people who needed his special magic, just so that they could move on. He could have been wrong about that, and Errante refused to answer, saying that "all Paths will find their direction in time." Rafe wasn't exactly sure what he meant by that, but he didn't ask. If Errante said they could go, they could go.

He now stood in front of the Big Top, as Errante came up beside him. The last few roustabouts were completing their duties, and Errante laid a hand on his shoulder. "Soon," he said. "Are you certain you wish to do this? It can be frightening to those who have never experienced it. That is why I always make sure everyone is asleep before I Travel."

"I'm sure," Rafe replied firmly. He somehow needed to see this, to see what his mother had seen when Errante had taken her from the only home she had known, to the place where he'd been born. He thought it might help him understand her, and somehow it made her spirit seem closer to him.

"Very well. We can go soon."

Around them, the Carnival grew quiet, and Errante closed his eyes. When he opened them again, he smiled. "I always arrive in the morning, but people never realize they miss a night. I transfer a bit of energy to everyone at night anyway, to make sure they are rested, even though little time has passed." He paused. "You must promise me one thing. Please keep your red coat on, no matter what happens. It has extra protections on it. Since you must step outside the area of my magic, it would ease my mind to know you have all that I may send with you."

"All right." Rafe was, in fact, still wearing the coat, not having returned to his quarters to leave it once his duties for the day had ended. "What about the others who are coming with me?"

Errante smiled slightly. "Do not worry. Persephone, Paul, Jim, Samson, and Nik have protections, both of their own and ones I have given them. But I have imbued your coat with some of my magic that you can draw upon if needed. If you are in danger, simply think *To the Carnival*, and you will all return to the gate."

Rafe had never realized Errante could do something like that, but then again, there had likely never been a reason. That Errante cared so much to come up with ways to protect him made him feel warm and loved. "Thank you. I hope we don't need it, but it's good to know it's there if we do."

"I hope you do not need it as well." Errante grew more serious. "Just because the last time we were here there was nothing that seemed dangerous, does not mean that is still the case. Please, be on your guard. I have wished a dozen times in the last few days that I had the household guard of my youth at hand to stand between you and any danger. But other than Jim and his knives, there are no weapons other than your own magic, and you are not yet trained in using it to fight."

"I doubt it will come to that," Rafe said reassuringly. They appeared to be alone, so he leaned in, pressing his lips to Errante's in a tender kiss. "I won't tell you not to worry, because I know you will worry anyway. But don't drive yourself insane with it."

Errante stroked his cheek briefly. "I will try." Then he stepped back, holding out his hand for Rafe's. "It is time."

Rafe nodded, placing his hand in Errante's, feeling his lover's warm fingers clasping his. All was silent around them, the night deep and dark, shadows deep in corners where the light of the moon didn't reach. For a moment Rafe thought he saw a flicker of movement out of the corner of his eye, but then Errante raised one hand, and the Carnival changed.

Rather than the solidity of wood and canvas, metal and glass, everything seemed to dissolve into atoms of light. For a moment it lingered in Rafe's sight, like a grainy photograph, but in colors far too intense to be represented on paper. Then the colors shifted, slowly swirling in the same direction as though they were in the center of the carousel and everything was moving around them. The light circled inward toward them, becoming like a cocoon, yet he could still see through it to the land and trees in the distance, and a lone pickup truck still parked in the field.

Then the ground fell away.

Startled, Rafe grasped Errante's hand more tightly. Around them, stars blazed in colors for which he didn't even have names, while towering, cloudy nebulas and distant galaxies glimmered with their own inner light. It was strange, looking down and seeing a world beneath him, and up to where the heavens spread out above in a canopy of light, endless in depth. He gazed around, awestruck by the beauty, and humbled, too, by the immensity of everything. It made him feel rather insignificant, as though the urgency he felt to find answers was meaningless in the face of... well, everything.

Below them, the world they had left had lights of its own, cities shining along coastlines where the oceans were endless expanses of complete darkness. It was breathtaking in its own way, to see the evidence of people shaping their world to their desires, pushing back the night as though raising a hand in defiance of the dark.

He looked at Errante, who was gazing back at him, watching him watch the universe. "You see this every time you move the Carnival?" he asked. "It reminds me of what I always see in your eyes."

"Yes." Errante smiled, gripping Rafe's hand more tightly. "I am happy to share this with you. I suppose it is too magnificent to keep all to myself."

"It is amazing." Rafe looked around, wondering what his mother must have thought as she gazed upon the immensity. Had she felt as small as he did? Had she wondered what her life might mean in relation to the entire cosmos?

He spotted something odd off to one side. "What is that dark area there?" It stood out like a hole in space, empty and menacing.

Errante looked in the direction he pointed, and his smile faded. "I do not know. I have discussed it with Persephone, but she says she hasn't Seen anything that indicates it concerns us. However, it is growing larger every time we move, so I am not convinced." He shook his head. "But that is a worry for another time. For now... let us take you to the world of your birth."

Errante stepped forward, pulling Rafe along with him. The universe *shifted*, a dizzying sensation of movement as though they had leapt across an immense chasm. When the motion stopped, they were hovering over another world. Unlike the one they had just left, there were very few spots of light, and they were isolated and dim. As the globe turned, however, stretches of blue ocean and green land peeked across the horizon. Rafe realized they were drifting toward the light, to the boundary between day and night on a continent where the lush greens of forests and grasslands gave way to the browns and tans of savannah, and the stark grays of mountains.

"This world has far less technology than the one we just left," Errante told him. Then he pointed downward. "There is the village where you were born. Come, let us take you to your first home."

Errante took another step. There was a shorter sense of movement, then they were standing on green grass. The sky overhead was a velvety dark blue fading to pinks and orange to the east toward the sun and melting into a star-spangled indigo and black in the west. Before Rafe could even look at where they'd landed, the energy that was the Carnival suddenly swirled around them again, obscuring vision. It was the process he'd just witnessed, but in reverse, as the light expanded, once again becoming the solid objects he knew so well. It was also different in this place, the Big Top shorter, the Carousel smaller and simpler. Metal trailers became wooden wagons, while the Funhouse and the Haunted house were no larger than a one-room cabin.

Then the sun rose, and Rafe looked out, for the first time he could remember, on the place of his birth. And recoiled in horror at what he saw.

"I am sorry," Errante said softly. He squeezed the hand he still held. "But I promised to bring you back as close as I could, so I did. This is the morning after we rescued you, so little will be changed, unless someone from another village happened by and summoned others."

Rafe nodded, but as he looked out at the horror, he felt a jumbled mess of emotions. Horror and sadness, fear, and even some guilt, despite accepting Persephone's explanation that the destruction here was no more than the reaction of a magical child when faced with a terror greater than he could deal with. He wasn't looking forward to seeing his parents in the same condition as some of the nearer bodies, but he steeled himself. Nothing had altered the feeling he had, deep down, that this was something he *needed* to do.

The Carnival stirred around them, people waking and coming out, though everyone had been told what was occurring and there would be no crowds that day. And while there were some newcomers who stepped closer, only to look out upon the scene and then hurry away, the vast majority of the inhabitants of the Carnival had seen it before, and had no desire to look at it again.

The people who were coming with him gathered. Gentleman Jim first, adjusting the brown duster he wore, which held many, many interior pockets for his knives. Then Nik, and Paul, followed by Samson, who was pulling a small cart behind him. On it were two simple wooden coffins and a shovel. At Rafe's questioning look, the giant man offered a sympathetic smile.

"I put these together for you. I thought you might like to bury your parents," he said in his soft voice. People expected a man his size to have a deep bass bellow, but Samson's voice was light and sweet.

"Thank you," Rafe replied. He moved to grip Samson's hand, his fingers disappearing in the grip of Samson's much larger one. "I appreciate your thoughtfulness. I am ashamed to admit it never even occurred to me."

"It's not as if you've been around death, Rafe," Jim said,

patting him on the shoulder. "Not in the Carnival. I'm sure you've read about it, of course, but don't be ashamed for not thinking of something that's foreign to your experience."

"The rest of us have seen death," Paul chimed in. "Too much of it, maybe. But we're here for you. You're family, Rafe, and we want you to know we're here for you."

"Indeed we are," Persephone said as she walked up. She'd changed out her flowing purple robes for a sturdy outfit of trousers tucked into boots, and a plain shirt. Her hair was even pulled back in a bun, something Rafe had never seen on her.

"Thank you all," he said, feeling his eyes sting. He may have lost his first family in this world, but he'd gained another one that was just as strong and loving. "I can't tell you how much this means to me."

"You will always be one of us, Rafael," Errante said. "No matter what."

Rafe wished he could throw his arms around Errante and burrow into his embrace, but he couldn't. So instead, he swiped at his eyes and smiled. "Thanks."

Errante gave him a smile in return, then looked at Persephone. "How is young Amelia? Still under the weather? I wish there was something I could do for her. But since it is not a sickness of the body, and merely a manifestation of her magic, there is little I could do, short of enclosing her in something that canceled out her magic completely."

Persephone sighed. "Unfortunately, this is part of coming into your magic as a Seer. I went through something like it myself, when the Visions coming in are so constant and you've not yet learned to filter them. I'm helping her through it, teaching her to compartmentalize them, and Peter has given her potions to help her sleep dreamlessly. Tia is sitting with her while I am gone, just in case she needs help. Otherwise, there is little anyone can do until she learns to *not* See when she doesn't wish to."

Errante looked grave. "I shall visit her, see if there is anything I can do."

"I'm sure she'd appreciate that." Persephone nodded, then looked at the rest of the small band. "All right, are we ready? We're here for you, Rafe, and we know where to take you."

With a last deep breath, Rafe nodded. "Let's go."

They headed out, and as Rafe stepped beyond the magical barrier of the Carnival, he glanced back to see Errante standing watch. He raised a hand in acknowledgement, then turned and followed along behind Persephone into the blasted landscape.

The Carnival had materialized just beyond the area of destruction, which had a circular edge that cut off almost perfectly. No doubt it was the limit of his power when he'd been a child, but the amount of damage was horrific. If he hadn't known the people had been dead already, Rafe would have been an emotional wreck at the thought of having burned people alive. But it wasn't difficult to see that everyone had been dragged out of their homes and executed, young and old. He wished he could bury all of them as they deserved, but with what seemed to be hundreds of bodies, he didn't think they could manage it without a lot of magical help.

It took some time to reach the middle of the village, which sprawled out across a somewhat hilly area with a river along one side. There were spaces between the houses where the burnt remnants of gardens could be seen. They had to wind around the bodies, and Rafe didn't look at them too closely. If he did, he might break down completely before they even reached his parents, were he to recognize other friends or relatives. So he set his jaw and kept moving, following along with the others who had been here before and knew where they were going.

Finally, they reached a house where walls still stood, though they were blackened and charred. It was a simple one-story structure, and a door in front stood open.

The group had moved through the village in respectful silence, but now Persephone turned to him. "Be prepared, my dear boy. It's… not pretty."

"Right. Given all this, I wasn't expecting it to be." He drew in a deep breath, then crossed the threshold, as the others followed along behind them.

And before him were the things he'd seen in his hazy memories. The room with wooden floors and walls, chairs knocked aside and broken. Inside, things were singed, but it was as though the damage had been far, far less in here. Save for small piles of white ash that dotted the floor around the single room, most things were untouched. Including the two bodies of his parents, whom he recognized at once.

His father lay on one side of the room in a puddle of dried blood. His throat had been cut. As he'd fallen, he had thrust out one hand toward his wife, whose body lay before the stone hearth.

Rafe trembled, but he forced himself to cross to his mother. She was curled up, and she almost looked as though she could have been asleep — except for the knife that protruded from her back. Unlike the look of horror on his father's face, she looked almost peaceful.

"You were sitting next to her. It was as though with her last breath she'd curled around you, trying to protect you." Persephone said quietly. He raised his head to look at her, and only then felt the tears that were running silently down his own cheeks when he saw the tears spilling from Persephone's eyes. "You were crying, but you held up your arms to Calliope when she knelt in front of you. She asked your name, and you said Rafael. Then when she picked you up, you fell asleep at once, as though you had been waiting for someone to come for you."

"Someone did come," Rafe replied, his voice ragged to his own ears. He knelt down next to his mother and touched her hand. "I'm so sorry, mother. I'm sorry I couldn't save you."

"You were little more than a baby," Nik said, coming to stand behind him and lay a hand on his shoulder. "And if you couldn't save her, you avenged her, and your father, and the entire village."

"How?" Rafe asked, looking up at Nik.

Nik pointed to a pile of ash. "I didn't notice those seventy years ago, but I would bet my magic those are the people who killed your family and slaughtered the village. You rendered them to ash. And they deserved it. Maybe you couldn't save your village, because I doubt you even under-stood what was happening. But you saved a lot more villages by destroying these evil people, Rafe. You lost your family, but you saved many more children in the future from losing theirs."

Rafe nodded jerkily. He could accept that, but it didn't make him feel much better. He returned his gaze to his mother. Her head rested on her left arm, and the right one lay on the floor as though she had been reaching for him. Yet her hand wasn't open; instead, her fingers were curled downward into a fist, and at the edge he could see something glimmer golden in the pale sunlight that filtered through the window.

His heart raced as he gently grasped the chain. He tugged, feeling a sense of pain for disturbing her, but something within him was screaming that this was important. Then the object pulled free, and he saw what his mother had been holding.

It *was* a chain, and on it was a pendant of a small golden

sun, rays spreading out from the central core. It was tiny, only the size of his thumbnail, but exquisitely wrought. He recognized it at once as being something his mother had always worn, though he couldn't remember if his father had given it to her or not.

As he held it, he could almost sense the magic in it. Surprised, he nearly dropped it. He didn't remember there being magic in the village, but he had been so young it might not have registered. But this pendant was out of place in these surroundings. This was the home of a farmer or a hunter. His parent's clothes were simple, obviously home-made, as were the surrounding furnishings. It was more likely this had been something from her life in Egypt, some-thing that had come with her across time and space when Errante had brought her here. He didn't know if it was good or bad that Errante only read Paths, not Fates; no doubt if Errante had known what he was bringing Neith into, he would have refused to do it, and Rafe would never have been born.

"I think... I think this is what I was meant to get," Rafe said, holding it up for the others to see. "I don't know why I didn't remember it before, but now I do. It was hers, she always wore it."

"It seems she wanted you to have it," Persephone said. "Memory is a funny thing sometimes, Rafe. Some things will trigger it, other things will hide it. Errante said you remem-bered parts of this when you heard your mother's name. More will undoubtedly come."

"It's magical." Rafe stood, looking down at it. "I don't know what, but I can *feel* it, like it's connected to me."

"May I?" At his nod, Persephone touched the sunburst lightly with a finger. "Protective magic. It's strong, too — as strong as Errante's magic and similar to it. I imagine she was trying to put it on you when she died." Persephone closed his fingers around it. "As any good mother would do. Keep it. Wear it in memory of her."

Rafe nodded. "You're right. I should." He slipped the chain over his neck and tucked it inside his shirt, where he could feel it warm against his skin. It was comforting, and it was almost as though he could feel his mother's love and strength touching him through the simple pendant. He had hoped it would unlock more memories. All he felt was the warmth of love, and it was enough.

"Is there anything else you want to take?" Paul asked, gesturing around the room. "Anything to remind you of your family? Family is important, trust me."

Rafe gave him a crooked smile, since he knew how close all the Galliers were. "I don't think so," he replied. He glanced around the room with its simple furnishings. "The pendant is all I need."

"You go on outside." Persephone pointed toward the door. "Let us move them into the coffins while you select a place for them to be buried. Then you can tell them goodbye."

He was going to protest, but at her firm look, he decided that she probably knew better than he did. So he went back outside, determined to find a place where his parents could rest forever. He might not have been able to save them, but he wanted them to lie together peacefully; hopefully whatever afterlife they'd believed in would welcome them, and maybe, through his actions, they would know he loved them.

CHAPTER 19

Once again, Errante was left to wait and worry when there was little he could do to help. It was not a position he enjoyed being in, but, of course, he'd done it to himself.

When he'd first started the Carnival, he'd only been thinking of camouflaging himself in a way Set would never recognize or expect. In the world they were on now, there was a civilization where such traveling shows were common. In the land of his birth, entertainers were often well regarded, welcomed for their role in providing a respite from one's day-to-day cares. Thus he'd begun assembling his crew, taking in people whose Paths led to him, or those, like Persephone, who were great of skill and wished to be elsewhere than their own world for a time.

But in tying himself so closely to the Carnival, using his magic to protect it and its inhabitants while simultaneously hiding within it, he'd inadvertently made it so he couldn't step beyond its border. For a long time, he hadn't minded it at all — what he'd seen of all the worlds before finding himself unable to step out hadn't made him any more trusting or happy than what he had within the safety of his creation. Every time he Traveled — still wrapped in the Carnival's protection — he had the entire universe to move through. He hadn't felt trapped, since he went to the worlds of the people he needed to help, and then they came to him. It had seemed like enough.

Now, however, he wished he could have accompanied Rafe, to be by his side and offer him comfort and protection while he faced the reality of his parents' deaths. He had hoisted himself by his own petard, and while he had some ideas about how to get himself out of the predicament, there hadn't been time for him to do more than think about it. So here he was, again, waiting and hoping that nothing happened he couldn't make right.

It had been only fifteen minutes of him staring out into the ravaged village, however, before Mario Gallier ran up to him.

"Errante, mother sent me to ask you to come," he said, beckoning Errante to follow. "She said Amelia took a turn for the worse, and she doesn't know what to do."

Alarmed, Errante hurried along after him, toward the purple tent. He stepped inside when Mario stopped and waited, then moved immediately toward the rear. This was where Persephone had her private space, where she rested and meditated.

"I'm so glad you're here," Tia said, rising to her feet. "This is out of my experience."

"Of course."

Errante stepped closer to the divan where Amelia lay. Her eyes were open, staring upward, and she was trembling. He sat down on the chair Tia had vacated and reached out to grasp Amelia's hand.

He'd intended to offer comfort, but before he could say

anything, she grasped his fingers in a viselike grip, sitting straight up and looking at him with wild eyes.

"It's the snake! It comes!" she said. "It comes for you, Khonsu of the moon. It has hunted you for all time, eating the stars, searching for you who have eluded his grasp. It is coming, for one in your midst has given it the power to find you at last."

With that, her eyes rolled back in her head, and she collapsed onto the cushions.

"What in the multiverse?" Tia's voice came from behind him, but Errante was frozen in place. Amelia's words held him as though encased in ice.

He could doubt nothing she said, for she had used his birth name, and spoke of things of which she could have no knowledge. Set had found him and was coming for him. And one of his friends, his *family*, had betrayed him.

Amelia slept as though in a coma, her hand now slack in his. He laid it gently upon the cushions; this was no fault of hers, and at least she had seen enough to warn him. Her sleep seemed natural, at least, and whatever was plaguing her with the visions was still beyond his ability to fix.

"I must go," he said to Tia, who was frowning in confusion. "Please, say nothing of this to anyone. I must make plans."

Tia nodded, then reached out to touch his arm. "I promise you, Errante, it wasn't one of *my* family," she said. "We appreciate the freedom you have given us from our curse. We all love you for what you have done for us."

"I believe you," he replied. Indeed, the Galliers had reason to be grateful, for the curse of their family would have made them all killers because of their nature. "Speak of this to no one, not even the rest of your family."

"Whatever comes, whatever threatens you, we will fight

with you," she said. "Just as you have always cared for us, we care for you. You are family."

"Thank you. Keep watch over Amelia and let me know if she wakes and says anything more."

With that, he departed the tent, moving back toward the entry and wishing with all his heart he'd never let Rafael step outside where Errante himself could not go. If Set was coming for him, they needed to leave this place. Perhaps he could keep one jump ahead.

The question was, how could he find out who it was? If there was a traitor in their midst, he needed Persephone. Perhaps she could See something that would lead them to the betrayer. Then he froze as a horrifying thought came to him. What if Persephone was the one who had done it?

Even as he tried to find reasons it couldn't be true — she had been with him since almost the beginning, she didn't know his true identity — counterpoints rose to plague him with doubt. Amelia had said his name. She could have said it before in Persephone's hearing. There was also the fact that Persephone kept reassuring him she saw nothing bad happening and said the holes in the cosmos were probably unrelated to him. Yet Amelia had spoken of Set eating the stars to get to him, so it seemed the holes were indeed from Set's pursuit. It made no sense about *why* she would have done it, but there was enough doubt in Errante's mind to leave him shaken. After all, she could have come across temptation outside the Carnival, and he would have no way of knowing.

Nik was another possibility. Could the story of the capacitors draining have been a ruse to slow them down, keep them in one place for long enough for Set to catch up? Again, there was the question of why he would have done it, but Errante found that paranoia, once triggered, was an incredibly difficult genie to put back into its bottle.

The more he thought about it, the more he realized it could be anyone. One of the roustabouts, perhaps with a charm that provided a false Path that had fooled him. Errante realized he'd once again been arrogant, as he had in childhood, when he'd believed his powers made him special. He'd thought the bond he shared with everyone he allowed within the circle of his magic was special, and felt the same way that he did. But he'd been wrong.

And that, apparently, was going to lead to his destruction.

The only person he trusted completely was Rafe. After Rafe's discovery of his identity, they'd been fully open to one another, their bodies, magic, and souls entwined in a way that left no doubts. No, Rafe would never betray him. To believe so was the way to madness, for then Errante would be left with nothing at all, and might as well end his life before Set even arrived.

He paced back and forth in front of the archway, wanting to scream in frustration as he waited, unable to do anything else. He needed time, distance, and Rafe's counsel. Surely if Errante had been blind to betrayal, Rafe could help him see it clearly. He had to believe that, or hope was already lost.

There was no way to make time move faster, and he worked himself up with ever darker scenarios. Perhaps Set had tracked him to this world, and it had somehow been a trap from the beginning. Rafael might even have been the innocent bait, if Set had discovered that Neith had been the one to Travel with him when he'd fled Egypt, three years before this point — or five thousand in his own time. Set was a manipulator, and anyone who would murder his own brother would not hesitate to slaughter a village.

Taking a deep breath, he talked himself back from the edge. Set couldn't have known the Carnival would come for Rafe. Not unless he'd already planted Calliope in the Carnival, for it was her Path he'd followed. And Calliope had left several years before. Surely if she had been the traitor, this would have occurred before her departure.

All these thoughts, and many others equally grim, swirled in his head. By the time the small group was visible heading back toward him, Errante was ready to weep with relief. He should have thought to send some means of communication with them, but once again, he'd been blinded by his own arrogant belief that everything would be fine and there was nothing beyond his control.

"Hurry!" he shouted. "We must go!"

He could see the alarm in their faces, but they ran for the gate, Rafe pausing to give Persephone a hand. Errante's pulse was pounding, and he was wringing his hands, wondering if their time — his time — was running out. As they came, he caused everyone else in the Carnival to sleep, not wanting to traumatize them more than he had to.

Finally, they reached the gate, staring at him in surprise and confusion. Rafe was the last to step inside, and then Errante shook his head at their questions.

"Join hands. There is a reason, and we must go now. I'm sorry about this. I suggest you close your eyes if you are afraid of heights."

With that, he grasped Rafe's hand in one of his, and dissolved the Carnival in a swirl of light.

He heard the gasps of his companions, but there was no help for it now. As the molecules of the Carnival surrounded him, he drew a breath, and the world beneath their feet fell away as they rose, higher and higher, into.

Nothing.

"What happened?" Rafe looked around as Errante stared into the emptiness that should have been the magnificence of the cosmos. But there was nothing but the world below them and its sun. The vast emptiness was far more frightening than the span of the heavens, and there seemed no place to escape to, no refuge now for him and those he loved.

Stunned, Errante looked everywhere, until he noticed a Path. It was dim at first, but grew stronger, bright against the surrounding darkness, a solitary beam that led off into the distance toward a single, far distant light. And where the Path began, for once, was at his own feet.

It was his Path, that he'd never seen, obvious now because there was nothing to keep it from his sight. And the star in the distance, he knew it, knew it well, for it was the one place where he'd always known his Path would lead him in the end.

The House of Geb, the world of his origin. The place where it had all begun, and where, invariably, it seemed fated to end.

Earth.

CHAPTER 20

Rafe gripped Errante's hand tightly, shocked by the sight of the empty heavens. Such a short time before, they had been filled with light and beauty, and now there was only a vast nothingness stretching in all directions. Persephone was clasping his other hand, and he could tell that she, too, was shocked. "What happened?"

For a few moments, Errante was silent. "Set." He said the name as though the taste of it was bitter in his mouth. "The enemy who has been after me so long that I can barely remember a time I was not fleeing from him. He has found me, and this is the result. Amelia had a Vision. She said he was coming for me because a traitor had given me away. Looking around me now, seeing the loss of all the Paths that once guided my steps, I cannot but believe it is true."

Rafe started in surprise. "How is that possible?" He looked around the small group as they hovered there. Every face was as full of horror and disbelief as he knew his own must be. "Who could it be?"

Errante shrugged, and there were lines on his face, the strain of what he was facing making him seem older. "I nearly drove myself mad wondering that, but I suppose it does not really matter, does it? But none of you need to worry. I will not let any harm come to you, no matter what happens. Do you trust me?"

"Of course!" Persephone said simply. "I always have."

"With my life," Nik agreed.

"Yes," Samson replied. "I owe you my life, and I will fight by your side if you allow it."

"Just let me at this bastard," Jim said, pulling a knife from his coat. "I know I said I wouldn't fight no more, but if he's threatening our family, he needs killing."

"I won't let anyone threaten you or my family." Paul's voice was full of venom, and his eyes flashed golden. "Let's go deal with him."

"Always," Rafe said softly, squeezing Errante's hand. "My Path was meant to be the same as yours, no matter where that leads."

Errante looked at them all, and his eyes were suspiciously bright. "Very well then, my friends. My family. Let us see what awaits us at the end of my Path."

He took a step, and the world beneath them flew away, while the one that seemed but a distant, faint light was abruptly closer. Beneath them was a different planet, one Rafe didn't think he'd ever seen before. But whatever it had been when Errante left, it looked as though it was a dead world now.

There were blue oceans, but on all the land that stretched from pole to pole, there was not even a hint of life-giving green. Everywhere Rafe could see was nothing but barren browns and tans, broken only by the gray peaks of mountains. Errante's eyes were wide with shock as he gazed at the place of his birth.

"This… is my world, but is not my world," he said, then closed his eyes as though in pain. "I can feel this is in the future, even from the many years I have been away. Because of him. This is Set's work."

"Are you certain?" Rafe asked. "Could one mage affect an entire planet?"

"Yes." Errante opened his eyes again, but they were dark and seemed almost lifeless with grief. "Set draws his power from the desert. From the movement of the sands as they bake under the rays of the sun, the rush of winds and the movement of the grains as they shift and slide. The more desert he has to draw upon, the more power he can achieve. I can only guess he did this in order to find me. It was once so green and full of life, but there is nothing I can do about it, at least for now."

With that, he took another step, and their small group was standing on shifting sands of gold beneath a sky so clear it looked almost violet. The Carnival began its reconstruction, spinning from light into matter around them. Rafe ignored the sight, since he'd experienced it before, and instead focused as best as he could on the surrounding land, looking to see if some horde of monsters or the creature he had seen in Errante's memories were charging across the dunes toward them. But it seemed barren indeed. All that he could see close were three peaks that raised above the sand dunes. They were only twenty or thirty feet high, but they were obviously made by the hands of men. If these were the great pyramids he'd seen pictured in the book, then time and sand were swallowing them up, and they eventually would be lost.

The Carnival grew still and solid around them, but the silence was like that of a tomb. The whole place seemed to hold its breath, not even the pennants that stirred in the desert air making a sound with their movements.

"Welcome, my friends, to what was once the glory of the land of Egypt," Errante said. There was a wealth of pain in his voice, and he gazed out at the pyramids with a look of loss.

"This was your home?" Persephone asked. "I sense it was once a land of remarkable beauty and power. There was once greatness upon these sands." She shook her head sadly. "So much waste. I can feel the sorrow here, as though the dead were weeping for the loss."

"All the tears of all the people of the world could not restore what was lost here or bring back my family and friends who perished on these sands," Errante replied. Then he shook himself and looked at the others with gratitude. "I hoped I would never set foot here again, but I appreciate your willingness to come with me, to fight beside me. Yet I cannot allow that, not for any of you. It would break my heart to know Set destroyed my second family as well as my first. I have but one thing I can do for you, and I will give it to you now." He pointed at the funhouse, which was once again the big, elaborate ride it existed as on worlds with technology. "All of you know of the exit door, and that it leads… elsewhere. There was only one place I could link it to this time, and that is, unfortunately, to the world we just departed. But I moved the time to a point in its history in the future from now. So far as I am aware, Set cannot travel in time. You will all be safe from him, to live out your lives without worrying that he will try to find you." He looked at Persephone. "You knew this day would come."

"Actually, I didn't," she said, looking distressed. "I had no hint this would happen! Something must have been blocking my vision. Something, or maybe someone? I failed to See, as I swore to you I would. I'll stay to do all I can to repay that debt."

Rafe took Errante's hand. "I'm not leaving you," he said. "I don't care what happens. We'll face it together."

"I'm sure as hell not going anywhere." Jim pushed his cowboy hat back on his head.

"Nor I." Paul said stubbornly, and Samson and Nik nodded their agreement.

Errante smiled weakly. "I cannot make you go. I can only beg you to do so. But please, if you will not save yourselves, at least get the rest of our family out, so they can be safe." He looked at Paul. "Especially your family." His gaze moved to Nik. "The roustabouts will not understand this. Please get them out, so they can find some Path better than the one I placed them upon. And go with them, if you know what is wise."

"As if," Nik muttered. "Fine, I'll get the rousties out, but as soon as they are gone, I'm coming back. I didn't get to fight the bad guys in my world. I was too old. But I'll be damned if I'm getting left out of this one."

Errante seemed to realize he was outnumbered and outvoted. He sighed. "I love you all, yet at this moment I could wring all your necks. But... thank you. Now please get everyone else away."

They hurried off to do it, but Rafe remained by his side, not trusting Errante not to do something brave and noble and stupid and maybe walk out of the Carnival to face his enemy alone.

"Who do you think the traitor could be?" he asked. "Certainly not one of our friends?" He watched as people ran toward the funhouse, herded by Nik, Samson, and Jim. Paul led his family toward it, but Tia seemed to argue with him. Then she threw her hands up in the air and followed. Darius was barking, helping to round up and herd those who appeared to hesitate. The stream became more orderly, but many people gazed back toward where he and Errante stood, obviously reluctant to go.

It horrified him to think that among the people he had

known his entire life, people he had laughed with, eaten with, celebrated with, that there could be one who bore so much animosity to Errante that they wished not only to see him dead, but given over to his worst enemy.

"I hate to think it is possible, but if Amelia's vision was right, it could be anyone." Errante sighed, running a hand through his hair. "Perhaps she was wrong, or seeing things incorrectly? That is my hope, but I admit it is likely a futile one. Set has always been clever."

"She was right about the book. I'll give her that, though I'm not sure even now what lesson I was supposed to learn from it. And it would take more than a simple girl from a backwoods world to put something over on Persephone," Rafe said slowly. He took Errante's hand again. "We'll get through this together. I refuse to believe that our fates would bring us together, only for us to lose one another a week later."

He looked out into the desert, watching the wind sweep the sand into spirals that danced and wove for a short time before collapsing again. Beside him, Errante stood stoically. "How long do you think we have until Set shows up?"

"I hope long enough to get everyone out," Errante murmured. "The only reason I do not move away from here to help evacuate them is that I want to make sure I can face him when he comes. I will not hide, and I have nowhere to run. For better or worse, it ends where it began. On the sands of Egypt." He paused, then squeezed Rafe's hand. "I will say this one time, and tell you, for the sake of my love for you, that you should go. This is not your fight, and it does not have to be your destiny. I would die happy so long as I know you live."

"It's my destiny too," Rafe replied. "And if you believe I could have any happiness in a life where I left you to fight and die alone, you are tragically mistaken." Then, throwing caution to the winds, he leaned in and kissed Errante, pouring all of his feelings, his support, and his belief into the contact of their lips. If this was to be their end, despite everything, at least Errante would know he was loved.

Errante kissed him back, and Rafe knew that whatever they faced, whether it was life or destruction, at least they would face it together.

CHAPTER 21

For a long moment, while kissing Rafe, Errante allowed himself to believe that perhaps everything might turn out all right. Then he pulled back, sighing, and raised his hand to stroke Rafe's cheek. "I do not have the strength to make you go, even though I should," he said. He could feel Rafe's certainty and see the determination in the firm set of his jaw and the flash in his dark eyes, and Errante knew there was no way to talk Rafe out of remaining.

"Glad to see the two of you finally figured it out."

Errante started, for once not having heard anyone approach. He turned his head to find Nik regarding the two of them with a grin. When he raised a brow, Nik shrugged.

"Look, I may be as asexual as they come, but I'm certainly not *stupid*," the engineer said dryly. "Figures it would take until the end of the damned world for you two to get together."

"It's not the end of the world, and we've been together for a *week*," Rafe said firmly.

Nik laughed at that, and Errante shook his head and stepped back from Rafe. "Are the roustabouts gone?"

"Yeah, and some of them threw a fit about it. Wanted to stay and fight," Nik replied with a shrug. "I told you that you have friends, boss. A lot more people want to stand by you."

"I appreciate it, but I cannot allow them to risk death when I could offer them escape," he said. It warmed his heart that they would risk everything to support him, but this would not be a battle for mortal men. He wished he could convince the rest of them to go, too, but he knew these people, and, deep down, he was grateful not to have to face this nightmare alone.

Eventually, the rest of the small group returned.

"Everyone seems to be gone," Paul said as he joined them.

"What in the hell…" Jim began, and when Errante looked at him in surprise, the big man pointed back toward the purple tent at the end of the Midway.

Errante turned to see Persephone approaching. She had replaced the sturdy clothing of their excursion on the previous world in favor of plate armor and a helmet. Sunlight gleamed on the burnished metal and flashed from the razor-sharp tip of the spear she gripped in one hand. She smirked at their astonished looks. "What? Yes, I'm a seer, but I was also a Valkyrie once upon a time. This isn't, as Jim might say, my first rodeo." Her smile disappeared. "Nor my first war between the gods."

Errante winced. He really disliked being termed a god, even by Persephone. "Not gods. Mages," he said firmly.

"Gods, mages, whatever you want to call them. Power crazed assholes," Persephone replied, waving her free hand in dismissal of the terms. "Just words. But now what do we do?"

"Wait," Errante replied. He looked beyond the Carnival gate, out into the desert toward the pyramids. "Set herded me here, but he cannot traverse time, or at least not as easily as I can. He may have gained some ability in that regard, so I will not underestimate what he can or cannot do. I went as far in the future along the Path as I could, though there was not much leeway, unfortunately." He waved a hand toward the desert. "This is in the future from my timeline, by something like a thousand years."

"So we may have to wait a while?" Jim actually looked disappointed.

"No, I don't think we'll have to wait long at all," Persephone replied. She pointed toward the pyramids. "Someone is coming toward us."

Errante looked where she indicated, and then he saw it. A form materialized out of the heat that shimmered on the sands. It was moving quickly, and then Errante could see it was flying toward him. Soon the figure resolved into that of a man.

He was of medium height, slender, with pale skin that the sun had not darkened, and red hair that almost seemed to glow like fire. He was dressed in a white loincloth, with a broad *usekh* collar in gleaming gold around his neck. In his hand, he held a *was* sceptre, and on his head, he wore the *sekhemti*, the combined red and white crowns of a unified Egypt.

He landed in front of the Carnival gate, his sandaled feet touching down lightly upon the sand. Errante stepped forward, placing himself between his enemy and his family.

"At long last, Khonsu." He looked at Errante with blue eyes as cold as ice.

Errante gazed back. After having lived in fear for so long, it was strangely relieving to lay eyes upon his great enemy at last. Set, also known as Sutekh, the lord of the desert wastes, maker of chaos and destruction. Now Errante simply had to defeat him, by whatever means he could.

"Not long enough, Sutekh," he replied. "I would have thought you would have tired of this pursuit long ago."

"Oh, no, my cousin," Set replied. From this distance,

Errante thought he could see madness in the blue eyes staring into him. "You escaped me, taking the power of your entire family with you. That cannot be allowed. No one escapes me."

Errante felt his family coming up to stand behind him, while Rafe took up a position at his side. Their love and support helped encourage him, and while he doubted he could simply talk his way out of this confrontation, he would try. If Set had truly gone mad over this pursuit, perhaps it could be used against him. Errante doubted that madness could do much to make him more unpredictable. Chaos had always been a part of how Set operated.

"Why does where I go or what I do matter?" Errante asked. He indicated the desert. "This is your doing, I would guess? You have all the power of this murdered world to draw upon. Why does my power matter to you?"

"Because I want it." Set said the words with complete calmness. "And do not weep for this world, Khonsu. You know well that everything tends toward entropy. It is one of the first laws of magic. I did little to make this happen. The mortals were quite capable of destroying it all."

"Really?" Errante looked at him, shaking his head in disbelief. "You wish me to believe that men did this alone?"

"I take it you never visited once you left?" Set raised a brow, then smiled, an evil expression that sent an icy chill down Errante's spine. "They bred like locusts, and devoured like them as well. Expanding and expanding across the entire world, consuming it as they went. One man might do little to affect Geb alone, but billions combined are as mighty in power as I. Perhaps I nudged it along here and there. A war or two, a few insane rulers, perhaps a disaster where I thought it might do some good. But all I did was to hasten the destruction slightly. The mortals were capable of doing the rest with no help from me. I, of course, was far too busy searching for *you*."

"Of all the power in the universe, you are fixated on me?" Errante asked. "That is madness, you know."

"Perhaps." Set shrugged, seeming unconcerned. "It took me a long time to figure out how to get off this world. First, I had to finish off the rest of my family, and that took some doing, but in the end, I destroyed them all. Even my father, the mighty Ra." He sneered. "By the time I finally found the old man, he was wasted and withered down to almost nothing, his power depleted in trying to defeat me. But if I did not receive all from him to which I was entitled, the humans were already busy expanding my domain." He pointed his sceptre at Errante, his eyes narrowed. "Now I will take your power as well."

"To what end?" Errante had to find some key to what drove Set to continue this madness. "Destroying me, taking my power, gives you nothing more than you have already, does it? You will still be the Pharaoh of a lifeless world that you helped destroy."

"Because I want more." Set raised his hands to the sky. "I want to be omnipotent, to go wherever I wish, to do as I wish. To go back in time and throw Ra off his throne as the first Pharaoh. To remake Egypt into a land that will never die, never be forgotten. I want to *be* a god as the mortals considered us to be. For that, I need your powers, so that I no longer have to rely on the devices of lesser beings. Which even you, for all your power, have had to do!"

Errante was considering explaining to Set that time paradoxes were a thing that no one, likely not even a mage of their combined powers, could overcome, when suddenly the air next to Set shimmered. Another man appeared — tall, lean, dark of hair and as pale skinned as Set. He was dressed in dark leather, and an elaborate horned helmet was on his head. Errante frowned, but he didn't recognize this person.

Apparently, however, Persephone did.

"Loki!" she spat, moving up to Errante's other side. He placed a hand up to stop her from crossing beyond the gate. She raised her spear, as though she would hurl it at him.

"Skuld," Loki replied with a scowl, then dismissed her as he glared at Set. "Lesser being? You'd be nothing without me, Set. It was *my* magic that moved you from world to world. My magic that blinded that bitch of a Norn. I'm the one who even came up with the plan to get something into the Carnival that they'd never suspect! To use one of their own people against them, and I did it so cleverly, the person never even knew they were being used!"

Errante straightened at that. If Loki spoke the truth, there was no actual traitor among his family. Any betrayal had been without their knowledge or consent, which was such a relief to him so great he almost wanted to cry.

But if Errante was relieved by Loki's words, Set was angered. "You were *nothing*!" he spat, turning his attention to Loki. "I found you, saved you from where you lay dying with that sword driven through your body, on a battlefield of a civilization in ruins! Remember that you swore your fealty to me, Norseman. I was old and powerful when your entire race was nothing but grunting savages scrabbling for food in a frozen hell!"

Loki didn't take kindly to the insults. He disappeared, then reappeared behind Set, a dagger in his hand. He stabbed at the bare skin of Set's back, but to his apparent surprise, the blow didn't fall. Set shifted, becoming a creature unlike any that had ever walked the Earth. He was shaped vaguely like a dog, but with squared off ears and a snout so long and thin that it seemed to belong to another species of creature entirely. Errante recognized this form, which Set had used in battle. It was as chaotic and disfigured as Set's soul, and belonged in no sane world.

Stunned, Loki whirled as Set crouched, apparently ready to jump at him. But a flash came from Errante's right side, and a spear shot out, piercing Loki's head and traveling halfway through it. Set staggered back from where he'd almost impaled himself; if he leapt a moment sooner, the spear would have gotten them both.

As it was, Loki collapsed, already dead. Set howled in rage, then turned to look at Persephone, who stood calmly beside Errante.

"He would have just taken Loki's powers for his own," she said, her voice utterly calm. "Now he can't. And anyway, he called me a bitch and fucked with my Sight. He had it coming."

Set transformed once more, back into his human form. The madness on his face was now not hidden at all. "You will pay for that! I shall have *your* power as well, harlot — yours and that of all those who stand with you!"

"You shall have *nothing*," Errante said. He could take Set threatening him, but anger rose as he made threats against the people Errante loved. "While you have been pursuing me, I have not remained idle. This is *my* Carnival, my family, and I have made it safe against you. I may be trapped here until the end of time, but that means you are as well!"

Errante used his magic to rid himself of the clothing he'd adopted when he'd chosen Errante as his name. Now he stood, clad much as Set was, in a white loin cloth, golden collar necklace, and sandals. Instead of a crown, his head was now bare and shaved clean except for a sidelock on the left side. This was how he had looked when he'd first left Earth. Now he was once again Khonsu, mage of the moon, and he stared back at Set in defiance. "Shall we battle, false-god? There is nothing left here to destroy in the land you have sucked as dry as your soul, so we needn't travel to any demi-plane. It is long past time for your soul to be weighed in Amenti. Perhaps you shall meet your murdered family there, and they shall have the vengeance they deserve!"

Set snarled in fury. "If that is what you wish! I shall destroy your precious Carnival!"

Before Errante could say anything, Set raised his staff, directing it at the Carnival. Light burst from the tip, but it splashed uselessly upon the shield Errante had long ago constructed. Where he could not step outside the sphere enclosing them, Set could not get in.

The flood of light continued, but the river of magic inside him kept the energy at bay. "You all really should go," he said, glancing at his friends. "I am uncertain if I really can keep him at bay for all time. For a long time, probably, but nothing lasts forever." Indeed, Set's power was far more than Errante had been expecting, likely because the desert surrounded them. He could sense the moon, as he always could, creeping up toward the horizon. Once it rose in the sky, he'd be able to keep Set at bay until it set once more.

"Not going anywhere," Nik said stubbornly. "I've got your back. My capacitors can help bolster any weak spots."

Jim was studying the shield. "If Perse's spear could go out, so could my knives. I could keep him distracted."

Paul looked at Samson. "If he gets through, we can take him hand-to-hand, right?"

"Right," Samson nodded in agreement.

"You can draw from my magic as well," Rafe said, stepping closer to Errante. "It isn't much, not compared to yours, but I'm glad to give it."

"We shall be fine for a time," Errante replied. "I have been reinforcing the protections on our home for thousands of years. And Set, for all his posturing, is not a god any more than I am. He is a man — really, more of a selfish child. He cares for nothing other than his own desires."

If it weren't for the fact that all their lives were at stake, Errante might even have pitied Set. He had murdered his family, including his own wife and children. He had also murdered any friends or allies and had done nothing but evil to everything he touched. When he was at last destroyed, Set would leave no legacy other than fear and hatred. His passing would be lost to the sands of time, even as Egypt was lost to the desert.

The energy directed at them halted, and Set stood, scowling at them. "You are stronger than I thought, Khonsu," Set snapped. "Or at least your magic is. But you have a weakness, cousin. If you will continue to hide within your creation and refuse to face me in combat, I shall simply have to resort to other measures."

"What other measures?" Rafe asked quietly.

Errante frowned, looking at his friends. "The only thing that truly matters to me is you, my family," he said. "I do not consider that a weakness."

A flash of movement came from behind the orange tent the clowns used. It was the structure closest to the gateway, and the back of it was hidden from their view.

A figure dashed from behind the tent, running toward the gate. Small and slender, she moved unerringly from the shadows and headed toward the arch.

"No!" Errante cried out, recognizing Amelia, stunned that she would try to leave the sphere of his protection, especially if she'd seen what power Set had brought to bear against it. He tried to put her to sleep with his magic, but somehow she resisted the magical command and continued to run.

Persephone moved to chase after her, impeded by her armor. But Rafe was closer and faster. He took off, with Paul and Samson only a few steps behind.

Time seemed to slow, and Errante moved as well, wanting to stop what was happening, but unable to move quickly enough. As he watched in horror, she stepped under the arch, just as Rafe dove to catch her.

They both passed through the gate, falling onto the sand at Set's feet.

"This is even better than I'd planned," Set said. One of his hands flashed out, and a burst of magic held Rafe and Amelia immobile at his feet. "Now, Khonsu, shall we discuss the terms of your surrender?"

ERRANTE WASN'T sure how long he stared, unable to believe that things had gone so wrong, so quickly. Set was smiling in triumph, and it was obvious he knew Errante would exchange his own life for those of his family.

"What, nothing to say now?" Set asked, his tone full of mockery. "See, I knew well that your weakness was, and always has been, mortals. I have no weakness because I refuse to let anyone or anything mean more to me than I do to myself. Do not feel bad, Khonsu — I brought down every mage in Egypt and most in other lands in this same fashion. I may have spent thousands of years getting to you, but it taught me much about your vulnerabilities. These frail mortals are not worth the sand beneath your feet, though I know you do not feel that way. So, an exchange? Your life for theirs. They mean nothing to me, and I am even merciful enough to allow your Norn to go free, if you just come out and face your destiny."

While Set was talking, Errante was thinking. He knew he could not save himself, but he didn't trust Set at all to honor any promise to let the others go. But if Set thought himself a master of deception, he was about to learn that Amunet, who had been stepmother to Khonsu, had taught him something of hiding his plans when he desired.

"You have won," Errante said. He bowed his head toward Set. He heard protests from his friends, but he raised a hand behind his back to still their voices. "But how can I trust you will let them go if I step out to meet you? Allow one of them to return to the Carnival, and you have my word, on my honor as the only son of Amun, that I will come out to you."

Set frowned, staring at him hard. "I suppose it does not matter." He gestured, and Amelia struggled to her feet. "She was a useful tool, despite being weak. I have no need for her."

Amelia was standing, blinking in confusion. Around her arm, Errante could see a snake twining over her wrist. With a cry she flung it away, but when it landed on the sand, it went inert, turning into a bundle of twigs woven into the semblance of a bracelet. As she staggered back toward the arch, leaving the Dryad's bracelet on the sand, Persephone rushed to meet her.

That was how Set had exerted his influence on Amelia, Errante realized, and learned the location of the carnival. Since the sticks had no soul of their own, Errante never felt the evil that Set's magic had worked upon them. There was no telling how many small traps such as this Set had devised over the centuries to ensnare him. Over the course of so many years, however, it was almost inevitable that one would find its way into the Carnival eventually. It wasn't even the fault of the Dryad, who probably never suspected that a serpent in his grove had, in actuality, been something far more evil.

"There! I have given you a sign of my good faith," Set said, crossing his arms over his chest. "Now come out, and waste no more of my patience!"

"I will. I simply need to say my goodbyes," Errante temporized. He bowed again, crossing his own hands at chest level in a gesture of respect. But when his fingers touched his collar, he did something Set would not expect or even realize he could do.

"Quickly!" Set snapped.

Errante straightened and nodded. Persephone was busy comforting Amelia, who was weeping. He turned to Nik.

"Don't do anything foolish, boss," Nik said quietly.

"Trust me, my brother," he replied, his voice pitched for Nik's ears alone. He removed his collar and pressed it into Nik's hands. "Say nothing more. Give this to Rafe, if he is allowed to return. If not, it is yours. I would tell you to use it wisely, but I know you will."

With that, he turned to Paul. "Be well, my brother," he said, taking Paul's hand.

"I still think we can take him," Paul said, but he pressed Errante's hand firmly.

Samson was crying, and he enveloped Errante in an embrace. Errante found himself lifted from the ground. "Let me go with you," Samson begged. "I might be able to break his spine before he can get off one of those spells."

"I appreciate the thought, my brother, but your Path goes on from here, while I fear mine does not," he replied. "Now, put me down, and promise that you will live and be happy. That is the way to pay me back."

"I'll try," Samson said. His tears fell on Errante's shoulder, but then he lowered him back to the ground.

Finally Errante approached Jim. Before he could say anything, Jim hugged him and whispered in his ear. "When you turn back around, hold for just a moment," he said. "Don't go down without taking the bastard with you."

Surprised, Errante pulled back, but then Jim gestured with his chin. Errante nodded, then turned, taking a deep breath as though steeling himself. As he did so, he felt something cold and sharp slip into the waist of his loincloth at the base of his spine. It tingled with a magic Errante recognized at once — the assassin's bespelled dagger. If he used it, it would fly true. He resisted the urge to smile; trust Jim to know a weapon that might help.

He might be heading out by himself, but Errante knew he was not alone. He carried with him more love than any man had a right to. And if he were to die here, he could face the scales of justice knowing he had done his best.

CHAPTER 22

Rafe lay on the sand, furious.

Not at Amelia — from what he'd seen and heard, the poor girl had been doomed the moment she'd put on that bracelet. He was fiercely proud of Errante for negotiating for her release, but he wished he could wring Errante's neck for giving himself up.

Well, if Errante was about to die, he wouldn't be going alone. But he was going to do his damnedest to make sure they both survived.

He couldn't move much, but he could turn his head enough to look back at the Carnival. He saw Errante saying goodbye to their friends, before turning and seeming to gather himself. Then he walked toward the gate, back straight, his chin held high, as though he intended to meet his death with his dignity intact.

"Finally!" Set's voice held exasperation and an overtone of greed. No doubt the bastard intended to drain Errante dry, then use his magic to gain even more power. Rafe may have been blessed to never have had to experience living under the influence of a megalomaniac, but Calliope had taught him enough to know that, to creatures like Set, there was never "enough" power. The more they got, the more they wanted, until they finally encountered something, like death, that even they could not overpower.

He held his breath as Errante stepped from beneath the arch. The message which had been there, 'Welcome Traveler', abruptly disappeared, leaving it blank. Rafe wondered if that meant that the protections around the Carnival had disappeared with Errante's departure. Somehow, he was certain Errante wouldn't leave those who remained behind without defenses; maybe it was to make Set believe that the magic of the Carnival was now gone.

Set was actually tapping his foot on the sand as Errante approached. When he stopped only a few feet away, Errante's eyes met his, and in them Rafe saw a strange sort of determination. But, more alarmingly, Errante's eyes were now… human. Just human, a dark brown no different from Rafe's own. Gone were the stars and galaxies that had always been there, as though Errante had left them behind in the Carnival.

"At last." Set's tone was triumphant. "Now, Khonsu, I will take what is mine!"

"One moment." Errante held up a hand and pointed to Rafe. "You promised to release him. Do it, or we can battle here, wasting the power you so desperately crave. If you do not let him go, you will not get what you desire!"

"You are quite demanding for a man whose life and power are forfeit to me," Set replied. "Rise, mortal." He gestured, and Rafe felt the pressure bearing him down into the sand suddenly abate. He rose to his feet, looking between Set and Errante, trying to come up with something, anything, that might save their lives. He could try drawing on his power, but it took time, and concentration, and he didn't think he had time to do much before Set would notice and kill them both.

"Go, Rafael," Errante said. His love was there in his eyes and in his voice. "Go back to the others. Set has given his word that you all may live. With that knowledge, I can die happy."

"No."

For a moment, nothing happened. Then Errante closed his eyes, as Set turned to look at him in frowning surprise.

"No?" Set repeated in disbelief. "He is giving his life for yours, and you say no? What foolish world birthed you, mortal? The affairs of the gods are not yours to meddle in!"

"Go, Rafael, *please*," Errante begged him. He had slipped one hand behind his back, and Rafe wondered if there was some plan in play that he didn't recognize.

"He had his chance," Set said. "I kept my word, and he refused, so now, he can..."

Set had been raising his hand toward Rafe, power crackling at his fingertips. Errante whipped a dagger out from behind his back and threw it with incredible strength straight at Set.

The dagger struck home, sinking to the hilt into Set's chest, right where his heart should have been. Set stared at it, then raised his eyes to Errante, while Rafe held his breath. Had Errante actually defeated his enemy so quickly?

But Set didn't stumble. Instead, a sound suspiciously like a chuckle burst from his lips, quickly escalating to a full laugh.

"Fool!" he said, shaking his head. He gripped the dagger, pulling it from his body and looking at it in disgust. The wound bled for only a moment, then quickly closed. "Did you think I battled my own brothers and sisters, my own *son*, and murdered my father without knowing how to defend myself? When I took my son Anubis's powers, I gained the ability to shift my internal organs to wherever I wished. Do you think I am foolish enough to leave my heart in a place where it would be vulnerable?"

Errante's eyes were wide; obviously he'd expected Set to die. As Set dropped the dagger to the sand, Rafe could even see why: the blade had been designed to strike true, and it had. Except that Set was a master of lies.

"This is far better entertainment than your Carnival could ever have been!" Set gloated. Errante's shoulders slumped, and Rafe ached for the expression of defeat that crossed his features.

"I am sorry, Rafael," Errante said, spreading his hands. "I would have saved you, but it was not to be. Just know that it was you who saved me. My love is yours through all the worlds and all the times, for it was you who healed my heart."

"Oh, how melodramatic is this?" Set said. He reached out, sneering as he grasped Errante by the throat. "Rapha-El — that is a name from the Hebrew slaves! God has healed. Their *god* died with them! I am the only god here, and this god destroys!"

Rafe was aware of Set's hand tightening on Errante's throat, then of the way Set frowned in anger. But the sight before him was suddenly overlaid with another. A sight triggered by Set's pronunciation of his name. It was the same way that his mother had always said it.

His mother's face hovered before him, her soft voice speaking. "Remember, Rapha-El. Always remember, my son, that you are more than you seem. You have another father, in a far off land, a great magician whose name is Ra. He has given you all he could, and sent us both away so that you may grow up in safety."

"What is this?" Set was shrieking. "Where is your power, Khonsu? Where have you put it?" He squeezed harder on Errante's throat, and the face of the man Rafael loved turned purple as he struggled to breathe. Yet Rafe still could not move.

Again, Rafe saw his mother. She lay on the floor of their house, reaching out to him, something golden glittering in her hand. He recognized it, the pendant she had told him that his father had given her, to protect her and him. "Live, my son, my precious chamudi. Remember, Rapha-El..."

Pain and fury lanced through Rafe. *Rapha-El.* Not just his name, but the last words of his mother in her native language, reassuring him even as she lay dying. Telling him she had faith in him.

And then he remembered what he had done, and how he had done it.

As his mother lay beside him, the sun had peeked over the edge of the window, casting a beam into his tear-filled eyes. He didn't understand that she was mortally wounded, that his father was already dead, but he knew she was hurt. Blood meant hurt, and there was a lot of it. And he knew the men who stood around them, with knives in their hands, had done it. From the way they looked at him, he knew they meant to hurt him as well.

The sun reached him, and he felt its comforting touch, the warmth and power pouring into him and filling him up the way his mother filled his cup with the milk he liked to drink. Then his mother spoke his name and told him to remember... just as the biggest man stepped toward him with a knife.

Fear, and anger, the feelings of a child who only knew his mother was hurt and that he was about to be hurt himself. He didn't want this, wanted this man and those with him gone where they could never hurt him or his mother again. Then the man had touched him, and Rafe had lashed out with all the power within him, releasing his anger and his fear — and watching as the men screamed, then were suddenly gone. But his mother never opened her eyes, so he cried again...

He opened his eyes now, looking at Set hurting the man he loved, and a hatred far stronger than anything he'd ever felt flowed over him. Instead of the light of a morning star barely breaching the horizon, now the full glory of the sun of Egypt, the land of his mother and true father, beat down upon him. It filled him, and it felt as if a dam had burst, a dam that had held his powers in check since his mother's death. He let it come, drinking it in, absorbing it into his flesh and bones until he felt he was overflowing. Then he looked at Set, raised a hand, and directed every bit of that power at him.

Light burst from the tips of his fingers, striking Set — his half-brother, he realized with some distant part of his mind — in the chest. Set screamed as the golden collar around his neck glowed briefly, before running down his chest in molten rivulets. Set stood rigid, his form dark within the beam; then abruptly, Set's body was no longer there, seeming to dissolve in much the same way the Carnival dissolved when it Traveled. The magical light, now unimpeded, splashed on the protective sphere of the Carnival, but did not penetrate. It dissipated instantly as Rafe dropped his hand. He breathed hard for a moment, his heart pounding within his chest as he stared at the small pile of white ash that lay on the golden sand. Then he cried out and ran toward where Errante had fallen when Set had dropped him.

His lover lay still in the sand, and Rafe fell to his knees beside him. The imprint of Set's fingers stood out on the skin of his throat, and he didn't seem to be breathing. Desperately, Rafe placed a hand on Errante's chest.

"Please... take my magic. Please, please, live. I can't live without you," he implored Errante's seemingly lifeless form. He tried to *push* his magic into Errante, but he didn't know how to make the transfer. That had been one of Errante's abilities, not his own.

For several moments, nothing happened. He heard shouts, and then Paul and Samson were beside him. He met their solemn gazes, seeing tears in Samson's eyes. To defeat Set only to lose Errante was the bitterest irony in the world.

Then, beneath his fingers splayed on Errante's bare chest, he felt a tingle. Slowly, magic flowed from his fingers and was absorbed into Errante's body. Paul spoke, but Rafe held up his other hand and shook his head.

"Wait," he murmured.

Above him, the sun still shone. It filled him anew, flowed through him, then into Errante. After a few minutes, Errante's chest hitched; he drew in a deep, shuddering breath, and opened his eyes.

Rafe cried out, a sound of happiness, and pulled Errante into his arms. "I thought you were gone," he said. "I thought I'd lost you forever."

"I am here," Errante replied. He put his arms around Rafe, leaning into his shoulder. "I thought I saw the afterlife beckoning, but then I was back." He pushed back slightly, looking at Rafe in surprise. "Set? Did I see you destroy him with a beam of light?"

"I did." Rafe pulled Errante close again. "I finally remembered what my mother was trying to tell me. It was the way Set said my name — the way *she* said my name. It brought it all back. My father wasn't Sachem. Mother was pregnant when she left with you. Sachem knew, but he married her anyway because he loved her, and she loved him. But the child she carried was fathered by the magician Ra."

Errante went still, then pulled back again. "That is why my mother said I was to take your mother away for Ra's sake. I was never certain what she meant by that." He relaxed, a smile of pure joy curving his lips. "It is over. At long last, after so long, it is finally over."

Rafe tightened his arms around his lover. "No, love, for

once I'm quite certain you're wrong. It's not over." He pressed a kiss to Errante's lips, then pulled back to look into his eyes. "It's just beginning."

EPILOGUE

"Are you certain you want to do this?" Nik asked, frowning in concern. "I mean, *can* you do this? It seems wrong."

"I can and I will," Errante replied. He looked down the Midway. "It's about time, don't you think?"

Nik raised a brow as Errante spoke, surprised by the informal tone of his speech. Rafe had been working with him on it; part of the magic of Ptah that Errante had absorbed so long ago made it difficult for him to think or speak more colloquially. But anything could be overcome with enough willpower, and Errante was determined to fit in now that he had reason.

"Still seems wrong," Nik muttered. "But I assume you're old enough to know what you're doing."

Errante laughed. "If I don't by now, my friend, I never will."

With that, he clapped Nik on the shoulder, then started toward Persephone's tent. He acknowledged the greetings that were called out to him and raised a brow at the wolf whistle from one of the roustabouts. Well, he looked damned good in tight jeans, if he said so himself. Rafe certainly seemed to approve, and that was what really mattered most.

He stepped past Gentleman Jim, who wore the Ringmaster's red coat with flair. He doffed his top hat at Errante, who chuckled in amusement. It had taken a lot of convincing to get him to agree to give up his duster and cowboy hat, but he'd finally agreed when he'd seen how good red looked on him.

After Set had been defeated, it had taken Errante a bit of time to recover fully. Having poured all his magic into the golden collar he'd left with Nik had left him drained, and he'd found he had to reabsorb it slowly. But within a couple of days he was back at full strength, and with no small amount of trepidation, he'd moved the Carnival from the blasted sands. Much to his relief — and that of Rafe and the others — the cosmos had been restored to its former glory. He'd Traveled them to the world of Rafe's birth and picked up all the rest of their little family, who had been overjoyed to see them. And even though he didn't tell anyone what happened, it seemed everyone in the Carnival now looked at them with awe.

When he reached Persephone's tent, he ducked inside, the cool, incense-laden air washing over him. Amelia smiled at him from where she sat behind the fortuneteller's table, shuffling a deck of tarot cards. Persephone stepped from behind the draperies, looking him over with a raised brow.

"Well, no one will recognize you as being with the Carnival," she said, then pointed at the shirt he wore, which was black and emblazoned with a large, stylized "NU" in purple. "What does that mean? It's certainly not the Greek letter, is it?"

"I believe it's a local learning establishment," he said, then shrugged. "Rafe said it would help me fit in."

"You look great, Errante," Amelia told him. "My world is like this one, so I can safely say you're good to go."

Errante smiled. He was pleased that Amelia had recovered fully from everything that had happened. It had taken her some time to stop feeling guilty, but eventually Persephone had convinced her that no one blamed her for what had happened.

"Thank you," he said, giving her a slight bow.

She laughed. "Okay, you don't fit in if you're going to do that. Just say thanks."

"Um, thanks," he said.

"You're all ready?"

"I think so," he said. "It feels strange, but…"

"But it's about damned time," Persephone replied firmly. "Don't make me get my spear."

He laughed and shook his head. "Please don't! Trust me, I hope you never have to bring that thing out again."

"Oh, I don't know," Amelia said, shooting Persephone a wicked glance. "I think she looked super badass. And sexy. Definitely sexy."

The Seeress raised a brow, but she preened a bit. "I did, didn't I?"

Errante shook his head. "Well, I just wanted to bid you… to say goodbye," he said.

"Goodbye?" Persephone replied, shaking her head. "You're coming back in the morning!"

"Well, yes, but…" Errante shrugged. "I'm new at this, remember?"

"True," she admitted, relenting. "Go on, then. We'll still be here when you get back, I promise. Even if I have to get out the spear."

Errante chuckled. "All right, have it your way," he said. Then he waved and stepped back outside.

The sun was just reaching its zenith, and the Carnival was

in full swing. Laughing people moved past him, the scents of popcorn and caramel apples filled the air. He could hear the barkers calling out their games, and over it, the sounds of shrieks from the Funhouse and cheerful music of the Carousel.

"There you are." Rafe moved up beside him and captured his hand. Rafe was dressed much like Errante, in jeans and a pullover shirt, though his was plain and dark blue. He looked just as handsome as he did in the red coat, especially when he smiled.

They started down the Midway toward the gate, stopping when they reached the arch. Rafe squeezed his hand. "Are you ready?"

"As ready as I can be," Errante replied. "What are we going to do on our date?"

Rafe laughed. "You'll see. For once, I'm the teacher, and you are the student."

Behind them, Jim's voice rose. "Welcome, Travelers, to Errante Ame's Carnival of Mysteries! What you see before you is no mere vagabond circus…"

Errante joined in the laughter, and together they stepped through the arch.

THE END

ABOUT THE AUTHOR

Rachel Langella and Ari McKay are the professional pseudonyms for Arionrhod and McKay, who have been writing together for over a decade. Their collaborations encompass a wide variety of romance genres, including contemporary, fantasy, science fiction, gothic, and action/adventure. Their work includes the Blood Bathory series of paranormal novels, the Herc's Mercs series, as well as two historical Westerns: *Heart of Stone* and *Finding Forgiveness*. When not writing, they can often be found scheming over costume designs or binge watching TV shows together.

Ari McKay is a retired systems engineer turned full-time writer and seamstress. Now that she is an empty-nester, she has turned her attentions to finding the perfect piece of land to build a fortress in preparation for the zombie apocalypse, and baking (and eating) far too many cakes.

Rachel Langella is a creative writing teacher who has been writing for one reason or another most of her life. She loves all things spooky and/or vintage, and she's given in to Ari's corruptive influences and learned to sew so she can make her own vintage-style clothes and costumes. Given she has the survival skills of a gnat, she's relying on Ari to help her survive the zombie apocalypse.

Visit Rachel and Ari on:
Website: arimckay.com

Amazon:

https://www.amazon.com/Ari-McKay/e/B00CHBT3NA
and
https://www.amazon.com/Rachel-Langella/e/B08JH
FY9J2
Facebook:
https://www.facebook.com/ari.mckay.7
And
https://www.facebook.com/rachel.langella.9

Twitter:
@AriMcKay1
And
@LangellaRachel

ALSO BY RACHEL LANGELLA

THE GUARDIANS OF GAIA

Blood Bathory: Like the Night

Blood Bathory: Absence of the Sun

Blood Bathory: Be Not Proud

ASHEVILLE ARCANA

Out of the Ashes

Forged in Fire

Quenched in Blood

Stop Dragon My Heart Around

STANDALONE

Call of the Night Singers

CARNIVAL OF MYSTERIES

Welcome, Traveler! Join us for a series of M/M fantasies by a talented group of both new and established authors. Whether you enjoy mystery, action, danger, or just sweet romance, there is something for everyone at the Carnival of Mysteries!

Kim Fielding * L. A. Witt * Kaje Harper

Megan Derr * Ander C. Lark * E. J. Russell

Morgan Brice * Kayleigh Sky

Nicole Dennis * Elizabeth Silver * R. L. Merrill

TA Moore * Sara Ellis * Rachel Langella